W9-CSW-891

Caught in her own web...

As the coach rattled on through the night, Alicia wondered if she would ever be able to extricate herself from the charade she had chosen to play. How she wished she had paid attention to her godmother, who had advised against it.

Now that she could not salvage the situation with Darcy and was facing a complete break with him, Alicia was forced to admit he was her ideal man. Although he was prickly at times, life with him would never be dull.

She had built more hopes on Darcy than she had realized. But it was too late....

LADY ALICIA'S
SECRET
RACHEL COSGROVE PAYES

Harlequin Books

TORONTO • NEW YORK • LONDON
AMSTERDAM • PARIS • SYDNEY • HAMBURG
STOCKHOLM • ATHENS • TOKYO • MILAN

For my daughter-in-law, Cathy Payes

Published April 1986
ISBN 0-373-31010-2

Copyright © 1986 by Rachel Cosgrove Payes. All rights reserved.
Philippine copyright 1986. Australian copyright 1986.
Except for use in any review, the reproduction or utilization of
this work in whole or in part in any form by any electronic,
mechanical or other means, now known or hereafter invented,
including xerography, photocopying and recording, or in any
information storage or retrieval system, is forbidden without
the permission of the publisher, Harlequin Enterprises Limited,
225 Duncan Mill Road, Don Mills, Ontario, Canada M3B 3K9.

All the characters in this book have no existence outside the
imagination of the author and have no relation whatsoever to
anyone bearing the same name or names. They are not even
distantly inspired by any individual known or unknown to the
author, and all incidents are pure invention.

The Harlequin trademarks, consisting of the words
HARLEQUIN REGENCY ROMANCE and the portrayal of a
Harlequin, are trademarks of Harlequin Enterprises Limited;
the portrayal of a Harlequin is registered in the United States
Patent and Trademark Office and in the Canada Trade
Marks Office.

Printed in Canada

CHAPTER ONE

LADY ALICIA Morgan Fitzhugh St. John allowed the Honorable Mr. Quincy Rawson to lead her into the rose garden. Behind them could be heard the strains of a waltz. Inwardly Lady Alicia sighed. She loved to waltz, and Mr. Rawson was quite a good dancer. Why couldn't he have put this interview off until after the ball? Still, it had to be gotten out of the way, she supposed. Perhaps now was better than later.

She glanced at her escort, dispassionately assessing his looks: tall; moderately broad shoulders encased in a beautifully tailored evening coat, the points of his snowy collar so high that he had trouble turning his well-shaped head; light brown hair cut à la Byron; steady blue eyes, steady expression. Quite a creditable figure was cut by Quincy Rawson, fourth son of the Earl of Stafford.

Gallantly Quincy seated her on a rustic bench under a bower of ramblers, then sat beside her, turning to face her. His countenance was stalwart, sturdy and dull. Alicia was a trifle disappointed in Quincy. For what she knew he had in mind, she expected him to be on one knee, hands imploring, presenting the best side of his profile for her delectation. Ah, well, poor

Quincy hadn't a modicum of imagination; nor had he ever read a modern novel, she'd vow.

"Alicia, my dearest lady," he said, his voice resonant and impressive, "you must know that I hold you in the highest regard."

Playing the game, she opened her sandalwood fan and peeped over the top of it. If Quincy was so lacking in discernment that he couldn't see that her eyes weren't the warm gray her intimate friends were used to, it was his fault, not hers. Nodding slightly, she let him continue his peroration, afraid that if she interrupted, he'd lose his place.

"Although unworthy, I cast my heart at your feet," Quincy intoned soulfully. Now he knelt before her.

It took all of her good breeding to keep from snickering. She pictured a bloody, palpitating heart snatched from his manly bosom and thrown at the tips of her satin slippers, dripping gore all over them. To distract her overactive imagination, well nourished by the popular novels she read so avidly, from this unromantic vision, she said carefully, "Yes, sir, do go on." Wicked of her, but she couldn't help it if he was such a hoddy-noddy.

"I adore you, dearest lady," he said, one hand carefully placed over his heart. "Will you be my wife?"

There, he'd said it. "Oh, sir, this is so sudden," she gushed dutifully, although clearly he had been screwing up his courage to offer for her hand for weeks. Alicia knew all the signs, having received her share of marriage proposals, all of which she'd refused. Even so, now that she was seven and twenty she was being touted as an out-and-out spinster, and indeed, if it hadn't been for her considerable fortune, Lady Alicia supposed, she would be getting no proposals of marriage at all at her advanced age.

Taking her inane remark as encouragement, Quincy rose from his knee, which he brushed surreptitiously, and sat beside her on the pine bench.

"I worry so about you, dear Alicia," he said, his voice thrumming with emotion. "All alone, with no man to protect you."

She couldn't ignore the opening. A wicked gleam appeared in her clear gray eyes. "I'm really quite capable of protecting myself, Quincy." Unable to resist temptation, she opened the dainty beaded reticule that dangled so fetchingly from her slender wrist and drew from it the deadly little pearl-handled pistol poor Papa had given to her on her sixteenth birthday. "Every lady needs to know how to handle a firearm, Allie," he had said. "Just remember, never point it at anyone unless you are prepared to fire it." With this excellent advice, he had proceeded to show her how to use it, making sure she had enough target practice to guarantee proficiency.

For a moment Alicia felt a twinge of remorse when she saw the shocked look on Quincy's face.

"Good God, what's that?" he cried in consternation.

"What does it look like?" she asked crossly, forgetting to play the coy damsel.

"It looks like a pistol." He reached a tentative hand for the deadly little toy.

Quickly Alicia slipped it back into the reticule. Tapping his hand playfully with her folded fan, she told him, "Naughty, naughty, Quincy, mustn't touch. You might get hurt."

"What are you doing with a pistol?" he demanded, all manly resolve and superiority.

"I'm carrying it to protect myself," she replied, her voice full of sweet reason. "Rest assured, Quincy, I know how to use it and am quite prepared to do so, if threatened."

"I knew you needed a man to look after your affairs, but I'd not realized quite how great that need was." His voice was stiff with outrage.

A cleverer fellow might have seen storm signals in Alicia's eyes, flashes of emotional lightning destined to strike him down.

"What's this nonsense about my needing someone to look after my affairs?" she asked with icy calm.

"Obviously old Wilkens is past it," Quincy blundered on, putting her frosty attitude down to normal missishness.

"And what has my father's solicitor to do with anything? Really, Quincy, there are times when I wonder what you have under that fine head of hair."

"I am referring to Wilkens not as your late, much lamented father's solicitor, but in his position as your trustee. You need a younger man to manage your considerable fortune, my dear Alicia."

This put Alicia's back up. Not even trying to quell the ire that she felt, determined now to give Quincy such a setdown as he'd never experienced in his thirty years of life, she said, vinegar on her tongue, "For your information, Quincy, Wilkens has not been my trustee since I reached my majority six years ago. I manage my own affairs.''

Dramatically Quincy struck his noble brow with the back of a graceful hand, a gesture Lady Alicia unkindly thought he'd probably practiced in front of a mirror. ''No wonder your affairs are at sixes and sevens,'' he cried, allowing a tremor to creep into his vibrant voice. ''Business affairs are the province of men, my dearest Alicia, not of women.''

''I've managed my fortune quite nicely, thank you,'' she returned, quite out of patience. ''It has increased considerably since I've taken it over.''

''Yes, you have a fine fortune,'' he agreed ingenuously. ''Together we could make it the greatest in England.''

Alicia tapped one foot in anger. ''Have you been looking into my financial affairs, Quincy?''

''Indeed I have, my dear. If we are to be wed, I must be well informed about the money that will come under my jurisdiction.''

''Imbecile!'' she snapped. ''How dare you pry into my fortune. It is none of your business.''

''But, but—if we're to be wed—'' he blustered.

''I'll have no more of your rodomontade.'' Not for nothing was there a Fitzhugh in her ancestry. Her Irish temper was now in full cry. ''I have no intention of marrying you, sir. I have no intention of marrying *any* man who wants me for my fortune.''

Seeing his dreams of wealth tumble down about him, Quincy forgot that he was a gentleman. ''You're already on the shelf, Alicia. Seven and twenty, and no husband. How do you expect to get one except with your fortune?''

It was too much. ''And I suppose you think you're a nonpareil!'' she cried, allowing a touch of arrogance to creep into her voice. ''Let me tell you something, Quincy. I wouldn't be Mrs. Rawson for anything. You're not the only one who's done some investigating of private fortunes. I have my own ways of obtaining such information. I know exactly the state of your fortune—it is nonexistent. All of your protestations of love for me are really protestations of love for my considerable fortune. I've never had any serious thoughts of becoming your wife. If there is anything I cannot abide, it is a fortune hunter!''

''Then be an old maid. Let them call you a spinster. I've honored you by offering my hand to rescue you from such a dire fate—''

''A fate far more palatable than that of being your wife. Oh, do hush, Quincy. Peddle your handsome but impoverished self to Cynthia Aldersgate. Her papa will settle a handsome fortune on her just to get her married.''

''Face would stop a clock,'' he muttered.

''A most ungentlemanly attitude,'' Alicia chided. ''But she's young, not on the shelf, as I am. A pity she's homely, but we can't all be pretty, can we?'' Alicia spoke with the assurance of a true beauty. She knew what her mirror reflected: a tall, willowy, shapely form; a head of gleaming black hair that fell like heavy silk when she let it down; a comely face, classically oval in shape, its creamy complexion touched with a blush of color; and her best feature, wide-set gray eyes as changeable as March weather. Behind the pretty face was a formidable brain, a combination many men didn't like. Her intelligence put Alicia at a disadvantage in the marriage handicap, for she was able to see through all of the fustian and rodomontade with which such exquisites as Quincy Rawson bombarded her shapely ears. It wasn't that she didn't wish to marry. She longed for a man who would sweep her off her feet and carry her away to be his bride. But this man must give her credit for having some brains; he must respect her for more than her beauty and her fortune. Alas, at seven and twenty, Alicia was beginning to think that such a man did not exist.

Precipitately she left poor Quincy in the garden to fume over her intransigent and unappreciative nature. That her harsh words were simply the truth never occurred to him. In fact, before she'd reached the terrace, Quincy had convinced himself that he had escaped a dire fate. What if that shrew, that virago, had accepted his offer of marriage!

Inside the ballroom, Lady Alicia spied her godmother and good friend, the Honorable Gisella Montague, sitting alone on the sidelines. Thankfully she took possession of the gilt chair next to her with a heartfelt sigh.

The Honorable Gisella, a formidable lady of advancing years, was known for her witty if acid tongue, her unconventional attitude toward life and her common sense. Although many years separated Alicia and Hon Zella, as she affectionately called her godmother, they were as close as sisters.

"Saw you go out with that fool, Rawson."

"And no doubt you saw me come in without him," Alicia said wryly.

"Dump him in the reflecting pond?" Hon Zella asked, giving her goddaughter a speaking sidelong glance.

"No—but I was tempted. Oh, the effrontery of him! He wants to manage my fortune for me."

"God willing, you sent him packing. If he got those gambling hands of his on your money, you'd be in debtor's prison in a month."

Alicia laughed, a mischievous look on her face. "I told him I'd had his financial resources investigated. Oh, Hon Zella, you should have seen his face—outrage personified. He should go on the stage. Think what an idol he'd be at the Drury Lane."

"You are a wicked young woman."

"Which is why we deal so well together, dear Godmama. I've learned my wicked ways from you."

"So you refused his offer."

"If he's the best I can get, I'll remain single, like you."

A shadow crossed the woman's aging, aristocratic face. She laid a velvet-soft hand on Alicia's arm. "Don't use me as a model, my dear. I'm not a spinster by choice. If my darling Harry hadn't contracted fever and died, I'd have wed."

"Surely other men..."

"I never loved another after Harry. It grieves me to see you alone, my dear."

Alicia felt faintly betrayed by her friend. "But surely you don't want me to marry one of these— these—"

"Of course not. Somewhere, though, there's a man for you. A strong man, wealthy in his own right, so you won't worry that he's only after your fortune." With a look of fond exasperation on her face, the Hon Zella continued. "Don't set your sights so high that no man on earth can come up to your expectations."

"Nor so low that I can't abide him?"

"That goes without saying. Now, go and dance with these young men. You're the loveliest woman in the room."

THE NEXT DAY Alicia was lost in a brown study. Her chubby little maid, Sally, crept about on tiptoe, hoping she'd done nothing to make her mistress so downcast.

Alicia was trying to decide how best to order her life to attain what she wanted most, a husband she could both love and respect. Obviously her fortune stood in her way, for it attracted all the wastrels in the country. She was also aware that her blunt manner and straight talk upset many men. They thought it unfeminine. But Alicia couldn't bear to simper and chatter like a rattlebox just to reassure men that they were superior to her. What a bore.

Very well, she must have some sort of plan. By now every eligible man in London knew of Lady Alicia Morgan Fitzhugh St. John's uncommonly sharp tongue. And her fortune was one of the largest and best publicized ones in England. How could she escape from her own reputation?

Sighing, wishing to forget her stupid predicament, Alicia picked up the latest novel by Lady D, the most popular writer of the season. Her stories were light and frivolous and her heroines frothy, with never a thought in their silly heads except to catch a handsome husband. Nevertheless, when she was unhappy, Alicia found herself avidly reading the latest from Lady D's prolific pen with something like pleasure. In this latest book, the heroine disguised herself as a ladies' maid in order to test her truelove's devotion.

Disguise. Maybe that was the answer! But how to accomplish something like that in London and the Home Counties when she was so well known?

Still, the idea had been planted, and over the next few days, it became firmly rooted in Alicia's mind. How could she become someone else? That someone would have to seem poor, if she was to get a husband who was not interested in her fortune.

Alicia sat down at the dainty white-and-gold French writing table, got out paper and a pen, and began a list of requirements for this nebulous project. Dipping the quill into the silver inkpot, she wrote, in a beautiful copperplate hand, "Escape." For that was what she planned, to escape from the cage in which she now lived, escape from the men who panted after her hand in order to get her fortune, escape from a single state into married bliss.

She would have to go somewhere far away, so that she would not be recognized. She must acquire a wardrobe of clothes suitable to a gentlewoman of meager means. How could she accomplish all this?

Perhaps—yes, she'd work! The fact that she'd never in her life had to raise a hand to support herself didn't disturb Lady Alicia. She set her mind to this problem and decided that she might find some ideas in the *Gazette*. People advertised positions in the paper. She might even place an advertisement herself. Position wanted. Gentlewoman wishes a position—doing what? Ah, there was the rub.

Alicia rang for Sally and asked her to bring the newspaper. Quickly she turned to the advertisements for positions available. Although she had attended Mrs. Simmons's Select School for Young Ladies, read French, played the pianoforte tolerably well and wrote a beautiful hand, Alicia couldn't see herself as a governess. A position for a draper's assistant was available, but the address was in London, and she was shocked at the tiny wage listed. Did women actually exist on such a meager living? As her eyes traveled down the page, Alicia began to be discouraged. She couldn't quite see herself as a barmaid, a scullery girl, a milliner's assistant or a companion for an elderly lady.

Finally she reached the very last advertisement on the page. Her spirits lifted. This sounded much more the thing: "Wanted, secretary for highly confidential work. Good character, good handwriting. Immediate opening. Write Thos. Nestor, Esq., c/o Rutland Arms, Bakewell, Derbyshire." Ah, just the thing. Derbyshire was far enough away from London for her to be sure that she would not run into any of her acquaintances. As to being a secretary, she certainly wrote a legible hand. The confidential work sounded intriguing. She would apply.

Then Alicia was forced to stop and think her plan through. As she wished to be incognito, she would not use her own name. On the other hand, she must present this Mr. Nestor with a character reference. Should she forge one? It was a daring thought, but one she quickly suppressed. He might well write to her false reference. Then she smiled. She'd use herself for one reference, and doubtless she could persuade Hon Zella to do a second one. Armed with letters from Lady Alicia St. John, Berkeley Square, and the Honorable Gisella Montague, of Grosvenor Square, both fashionable London addresses, she would surely be able to obtain this enticing position.

Now for her name. Alicia went through a number of possibilities, discarding them all for reasons both sound and frivolous. Finally she hit on the perfect solution. If her employer should somehow discover her sham, she could honestly say that she was using her own name. She was Lady Alicia Morgan Fitzhugh St. John, her two middle names courtesy of Welsh and Irish forebears. She would call herself Morgan Fitzhugh.

Holding the quill between her index and second fingers, so as to disguise her writing, and taking pains not to write in her usual clear hand, she penned a reference for Morgan Fitzhugh, mentioning intelligence, good character, good handwriting. She was careful not to make the letter too glowing, yet she made a point of adding that she was sorry to lose the good offices of

Fitzhugh, who was leaving her employ because the air of London was unsalubrious. The last fact was no lie.

Next she wrote the letter of application, stressing her immediate availability. Then she rang for Sally, saying she was going calling. After a brief consultation, Sally laid out a lilac silk walking dress with long, fitted sleeves and brought a matching purple velvet spencer and bonnet from the wardrobe. Kid slippers and gloves completed her outfit.

"Will it rain?" she worried. "Should I take a parasol?"

"It's a fine May day, your ladyship. Of course, a shower can always blow up in May." Sally went back to the wardrobe and brought out a fine parasol of pale lilac oiled silk. "Better be safe than sorry, milady."

Being such an independent lady, Alicia chose to stroll alone from her elegant town house on Berkeley Square along Mount Street to Carlos Place, and thence to her godmother's equally charming abode on Grosvenor Street. Why take Sally away from her other duties just to walk this short distance with her?

Fortunately her elderly friend was at home and did not have other morning callers. Over chocolate served in Hon Zella's best Minton cups, Alicia outlined her plan.

Expecting her adventurous, spirited godmother to fall in with her scheme, Lady Alicia was surprised to find her totally opposed.

"Alicia, it just won't do, my girl. Think of your reputation."

Alicia laughed lightly. "When you're an heiress, you can do as you please, Hon Zella. You know that."

Her godmother was not persuaded. "My dear, it is not only sheer folly to embark on such a scatterbrained course, it is also dangerous. Who is this Thomas Nestor, Esquire? He might be a murderer, for all you know."

"More likely he's some kindly old gentleman who needs help writing his dull memoirs. You can't dissuade me, Hon Zella. I am quite determined to go."

"And you expect to find a husband this way? If you masquerade as a gentlewoman of meager means, you'll attract the local butcher, my dear. It's a harebrained scheme."

Alicia sighed. "I must do something, dearest godmother. I can't go on regarding with suspicion every man who smiles at me and seeing gold guineas in his eyes. Remember, I'm seven and twenty, and life is passing me by. I can buy myself a husband any day of the week. Would you want that fate for me?"

"No, Alicia, not that. But this proposal is so...drastic."

"Drastic situations require drastic measures. I am quite decided. Will you help me by writing me a reference? You'll be the only person who knows where I'll be, and I promise to write to you once I'm ensconced in Derbyshire."

Her godmother had never been able to resist Alicia when she used that honeyed, wheedling tone. Reluctantly she agreed.

"Wicked woman, ring for my maid. I'll write you a letter; but I do it against my better judgment."

Alicia kissed the soft old cheek. "You are my dearest friend, Hon Zella. I shan't do anything to disgrace the name of St. John."

CHAPTER TWO

THE COACH GUARD played a lilting tune on his long brass trumpet, and Lady Alicia breathed a prayer of thanks that the journey was ended. She ached in every bone, and her poor bottom must be bruised black and blue. As speed was of the essence, she had come by Royal Mail, but though the mail coach was fast, it wasn't overcomfortable.

With shrill of brake and creaking of harness, the coach pulled up in front of the Rutland Arms in the charming village of Bakewell. As Alicia put a well-shod foot on the step the guard had placed for the convenience of the passengers, she felt she might collapse from fatigue. She felt grimy from the long journey, crowded into the swaying coach, during which she had sometimes almost wished she were riding on top, where the air was fresher than the smelly box in which she was trapped for two interminable days. They had stopped at the King's Head in Coventry on the first night, and she'd been lucky enough to get a bedroom to herself by paying an exorbitant rate for a tiny chamber under the eaves. Although she now was pretending to be a gentlewoman of few means, she drew the line at sleeping with a stranger. At least her bed, lumpy and hard, had been free of bugs.

Now the really tricky part of her adventure would start. It seemed impossible that only a week had passed since she answered Mr. Nestor's advertisement. She'd had a reply by return mail, offering her the position if she would come immediately, as speed was of the utmost importance. The awkward part of the letter from Mr. Nestor was the salutation; "Dear Sir." Alicia expected there would be some repercussions when Mr. Nestor saw she was a woman; but she had his letter safe in her cloth reticule, and she would insist on being given a chance at the position before she was dismissed for being female. It was not her fault if they mistook her name. Of course, she had been careful in wording her letter of recommendation for Morgan Fitzhugh, and she'd cautioned her godmother to be equally clever in avoiding any hint of Morgan Fitzhugh's gender.

"Alicia, I don't like it," Hon Zella had said.

She'd ignored her godmother's loving advice, and here she was, feeling as bespattered and besmirched as the black-and-maroon Royal Mail coach from which she was descending. It had gleamed so brightly when she'd caught it at Portland Street in London. Now its appearance lowered her already flagging spirits. Perhaps Hon Zella had been right. This might be a disastrous mistake. Then Alicia straightened her spine and put a smile on her face. She would not be defeated before she even started.

The Rutland Arms was an important coaching inn built at the intersection of two roads. It was a new building, quite elegant, its dignified white portico contrasting with red walls and a slate roof, its square chimneys topped with tile chimney pots. It stood on the site of an older coaching inn dating from the past century.

After making sure that her boxes had been taken from the top of the coach and set in front of the inn door, Alicia took a deep breath and went inside. Her future lay here in the Rutland Arms with the unknown Thomas Nestor, Esquire. She only wished she could bathe and change out of her travel-stained gown of plain brown stuff, which her clever dressmaker had whipped up almost overnight. Over it she wore a pelisse of light Highland wool in a heather tweed, and she'd topped the traveling outfit with a small bonnet of dark straw tied with grogram ribbons. She hoped she looked the part of a reliable lady in reduced circumstances.

In the hall, she told the innkeeper, "I am Miss Morgan Fitzhugh. I am to meet Mr. Thomas Nestor here."

The innkeeper, an obese man with a florid complexion and sparse hair tied at his neck with a greasy string, looked surprised, eyeing her openly.

Annoyed at this bold attention, Alicia used the tone she'd perfected in years of dealing with servants. "Is Mr. Nestor expecting me?"

The vulgar fellow gave a guffaw, which further incensed her, before he said, a snicker in his voice, "I daresay you'll be a surprise to him, Miss Fitzhugh."

Looking down her nicely formed patrician nose, Alicia said in icy tones, "He is expecting me."

With a sly grin, the man countered, "I wouldn't be too sure of that, ma'am."

Exasperated now beyond all tolerance, because she was uncommonly wearied from the hurried journey, Alicia asked sharply, "Is he or is he not here?"

Just then the door from outside opened, and Alicia heard a soft feminine voice asking, "Is anything the matter, Kilrock?"

Alicia turned to face a tall, dark-haired woman with a rather sweet face who smiled at her. "You seem to be having some difficulty," she said apologetically. "I didn't mean to intrude."

The woman's eyes were keenly intelligent, and Alicia immediately felt at ease with her. "I am to meet someone here, but this—" she hesitated, then decided not to call Kilrock an oaf—"man is being most obtuse."

The woman turned to the innkeeper and asked quietly, "What is the trouble, Kilrock?"

"Uh, nothing, Miss Austen," he muttered, abashed. "The lady is looking for Mr. Nestor, from Pennsfield Manor, and he's a bit late arriving." With a touch of whine in his words, Kilrock added, "I told him what time the mail gets here. Set your clocks by the mail coach."

"Ah, I see a coach coming up Matlock Street now." The woman smiled at Alicia, adding politely, "If your business allows, perhaps you can take a dish of tea with me later. I am Miss Jane Austen, and I'm staying on the first floor this summer."

Alicia caught herself just in time. She had almost introduced herself as Lady Alicia St. John. "And I'm Morgan Fitzhugh. Thank you for your kind invitation to tea, Miss Austen. I cannot give you a firm reply until I see Mr. Nestor, as I am here on business."

They parted with polite nods, and the lady went up the staircase to her room.

Properly chastened, the innkeeper suggested that Alicia might prefer to wait in a private parlor. "I'll have Mr. Nestor join you when he comes in, miss. Would you want tea?"

Much as she wanted a cup of hot tea, Alicia thought it better to wait. She had considerable trepidation about this interview.

Minutes later there was a tap at the door, a very discreet sound, the kind of rap a servant makes before entering a chamber. When she called, "Come in," the door was opened, and a man of middle years entered the parlor. He was short and wiry, his graying hair pulled back and clubbed at his neck with a bit of dark ribbon. His clothing was unobtrusive, although of good fabric and cut. He had removed his hat, and now he bowed politely. "Are you Morgan Fitzhugh?" he asked.

She gave a slight curtsy and nodded. "I am. Mr. Nestor?"

"Yes, I'm Thomas Nestor." He eyed her almost belligerently. "There's been a horrible mistake, Miss Fitzhugh."

Here it came. Alicia braced herself for trouble. "A mistake? I don't understand, Mr. Nestor."

"We were expecting a gentleman, of course, miss. I'm not sure what his lordship will say. Probably he'll fly into a rage, as he needs a secretary so desperately."

"That's what I'm here to provide." Alicia forced herself to keep her voice even so as not to show how perturbed she was.

"I'm afraid it won't do at all," Mr. Nestor muttered.

"Am I to understand that you are not my employer?" she insisted, taking matters into her own hands. Alicia had never been one to mince words. "You mention his lordship. What is his lordship's name?"

"I'm not at all sure I should say, miss, seeing as how you're a young woman."

"Sir," she replied frostily, "I have rushed from London at your behest." She opened her reticule and fished out the letter confirming her position. "I seem to have been grossly misled. I thought Mr. Nestor needed a secretary."

He looked pained. "It is a very confidential matter, Miss Fitzhugh."

"I am quite capable of handling confidential matters, my good man." Now she used the tone she employed when giving one of her suitors a setdown. "I can see that, for some reason, your employer has kept his name a secret from me. I daresay he must have some excellent reason for this—" she paused just a breath "—strange behavior. As it really is he who has hired me, not you, I suggest that we suspend these nonsensical maneuverings until I am face-to-face with him."

She saw Nestor's lips tighten. He wasn't used to being talked to in this fashion. If he was only a servant, which she now suspected, then he must be near the top of the hierarchy in his establishment—butler or valet. She'd guess valet. "Is his lordship to join us here?" She eyed Nestor intently. "If so, then we shall order tea. I have come on a long, hurried journey. I was led to believe that speed was of the utmost importance."

"Indeed it is, miss."

"Then stop shilly-shallying, Mr. Nestor. Do I see your employer here or elsewhere?"

She saw him waver. Then Nestor capitulated. "His lordship is waiting at Pennsfield Manor," he conceded. "It is nearby. Tea will be served there."

"I should hope so."

Alicia was having second thoughts about this escapade. Maybe Hon Zella was right. Perhaps it was harebrained of her to go traipsing off to the wilds of Derbyshire to some unknown fate. Now she worried about the nature of this confidential work she was to transcribe. Perhaps it was indecent in nature.

Slipping the ribbons of her reticule over her wrist, Alicia picked up the small portmanteau in which she had put her immediate requirements for the journey, including the romance by Lady D that she'd thought she might read during the long, dreary coach ride. Unfortunately, the road was so rough that it was impossible to read while they jounced along. Well, no great loss. It was a silly story.

Wishing for a cup of tea, sorry now she'd not availed herself of the pleasant Miss Austen's hospitality, Alicia followed Nestor out of the Rutland Arms.

"Are these your boxes?" he asked, pointing to her luggage, which the guard had piled beside the door to the inn.

"They are."

Nestor motioned to the coachman who sat on the box of a shiny landaulet. Alicia, who appreciated fine horseflesh, glanced with admiring eyes at the matched bays harnessed to it. Obviously her new employer had plenty of the blunt. She allowed herself a tiny daydream. Perhaps he would be the man she'd been waiting for these many years.

Nestor handed her into the coach, then sat facing her.

"Now, what is the name of my new employer?" she asked.

Nestor hesitated, then said, "Perhaps it would be better if you discussed everything with his lordship, ma'am."

"Oh, don't be such a fool," she cried in exasperation. "All you've done since I arrived is to try to gammon me. As I'm to meet this mysterious lordship, surely I can know his name. Or do you prefer that I complain about your treatment of me the moment I lay eyes on him?" Ah, that got in, just as she thought it would. Servants don't like complaints laid against them with their masters.

"He is Darcy Cummings, Baron Pennsfield," Nestor said grudgingly. "And we travel to his estate, Pennsfield Manor, which is about two miles from Bakewell."

"And why all the mystery?" she asked; but even as she did, there was something about the name Pennsfield that rang a faint bell. She couldn't recall where she'd heard it before. She'd write to Hon Zella, who was a walking encyclopedia of information about the nobility. If there was a story about Pennsfield, and Alicia was sure there was, Hon Zella would know it.

"I think it best if his lordship talk with you" was all Nestor would say. He retreated into silence, leaving Alicia to endure the motion of the coach. Although it was a pleasant enough drive through charming countryside, she was by now so tired of coaches that she would almost have preferred to work in the kitchen of the Rutland Arms than travel farther to this new position, which sounded worse by the moment. If only she could remember why the name Pennsfield seemed familiar. A scandal? That was the most likely explanation. Obviously, she'd not get any information out of the taciturn Nestor.

Hoping to shock him into speech, Alicia said, "I presume that you are Lord Pennsfield's valet."

He gave her a baleful stare. "I am."

If she'd hoped to get into a conversation with him, she was sorely disappointed. Very well, she would wait until she had Lord Pennsfield under her scrutiny. He was probably fat and fifty, perhaps given to strong drink. Or he might be the type who find women fair game. No doubt he thought himself irresistible. Well, he'd discover that Lady Alicia Morgan Fitzhugh St. John was made of stern stuff. She'd give him the setdown of his life if he tried to become familar with her.

Now she began to appreciate Hon Zella's misgivings. Perhaps she'd been too bold. A lecher might see her conduct as an invitation to take liberties. Just let him try. She had her little pearl-handled pistol in her reticule. Of course, the roads were essentially safe nowadays, the highwaymen of the previous century only history; but occasionally a robber did hold up a coach. She meant to be ready for all contingencies.

Now the coach turned off the main road and drove through a handsome gateway hung with ornate iron gates. It proceeded along a drive lined with lime trees in leaf, with well-kept parkland on either side. Alicia's practiced eye noted all the details, and her spirits rose. At least she would not be working in some old ruin of a house with drafts freezing her feet and the back of her neck.

"Almost there, Miss Fitzhugh," Nestor said, breaking the long silence. Loosening up slightly, he added, "I daresay you are glad your journey is over. It is unfortunate that you'll have to return to London."

"Why should I do that?" she snapped. "If his lordship plans to be in London, why ask me to make this tiring journey?"

She saw consternation on his lined face. "It's just that he'll not find you suitable, miss. He expects a man."

"I can write quite as legibly as any man" was her cold rejoinder. "He advertised for a secretary. He did not say the secretary must be a man. He has hired me, and I expect him to keep his bargain."

"We'll see," Nestor muttered.

"Yes, we shall see," she retorted, her voice peppery.

The drive curved, the road going up a slight incline. Then the trees opened up, and before her, on a little knoll, Alicia saw a charming Palladian mansion built of light gray stone. Curved colonnades extended on either side of the main block, and smaller wings were placed at the end of each semicircle. The proportions were classic; the entire facade was elegant. Silhouetted against the late afternoon sky, Pennsfield Manor presented a picture of wealth and privilege.

"How lovely," she exclaimed.

"It's built on the site of a much older manor house," Nestor explained, warming a bit to her enthusiasm. "The barony is very old."

And so, no doubt, was the baron, Alicia thought wryly.

The coach swept up a graveled court to the Ionian pillars of the portico, and a footman in silver-and-gray livery hurried out to let down the steps for Alicia. She was pleased with the appearance of the place. Now if only her future employer was as pleasant as his home, she'd be happy.

Nestor ushered her past a butler more regal-looking than the princes. "Where is his lordship?" he asked the austere factotum.

"In his study," the elderly butler murmured, "ringing every five minutes to see if you and the new gentleman have arrived." Then he added sotto voce, "Where is the new secretary—and who might this female person be?"

Alicia, whose hearing was keen, turned a withering look on the butler and announced plainly, "I am the secretary." It did her heart good to see shock on the man's face before he remembered that butlers never show emotion and wiped his face clean of all but a supercilious expression.

It was at this moment that another character burst on the scene. He was tall, slender and elegant, with pale blond hair that waved almost to his collar, with one errant lock falling over a noble brow. He was clad in a plain jacket and fawn trousers that fitted him snugly. With them he wore low Hessians of the finest leather, well polished, a tribute to Nestor's care.

The most interesting thing about his appearance was his right arm, encased in a splint and suspended in a sling of black silk.

The gentleman looked to be in his late thirties and was perhaps the handsomest man Alicia had ever seen. He was also one of the angriest, his bright blue eyes snapping with annoyance as he strode over to their side of the great hall.

"Where have you been, Nestor?" he raged. "And where is that Fitzhugh fellow? I'm falling further and further behind my timetable." Then, as if noticing Alicia for the first time, he stopped short, looked her up and down as if she were a filly at the Horncastle horse fair, and demanded severely, "And who might you be, madam?"

Dropping a minimal curtsy, then looking him in the eye, she announced, "I, my lord, am Morgan Fitzhugh. If you are Lord Pennsfield, I believe I am to work for you." Thinking attack might be best, for she could see his face darken with rage, Alicia added quickly, "Although my letter of employment states that I am to be secretary to Mr. Nestor."

"What fustian is this?" Lord Pennsfield roared. For all his slender build, he possessed a voice that could easily have commanded a regiment. He walked up to Alicia, pointed a finger of his left hand at her and said, "You're not a man."

"Indeed, sir, you are correct. I am not." She stood her ground.

"But I assumed from your name that you were a man."

"I am sorry, my lord, that I cannot oblige you by changing my gender. I am Morgan Fitzhugh, the person employed to be a secretary and to handle certain confidential matters. I assure you that I write a clear hand and that I am exceedingly discreet."

"It won't do. It won't do at all," his lordship said. "I was expecting a male secretary, naturally. A female might be employed by a lady to write her letters, but a secretary employed by a gentleman of course must be a man."

"And pray tell me what advantage there is to being a man when it comes to transcribing chicken scratches into legible writing?" Lady Alicia asked with spirit. "I know more women who write a fine hand than I do men."

"I didn't want a female secretary," he insisted, his voice now dangerously low.

She fished in her reticule, bringing out the original advertisement that she had clipped from the *Gazette*. "No gender is stipulated in this advertisement, sir. All it requires is a good character and good handwriting. I sent you two character references, which you obviously accepted, else I should not now be standing here in this drafty hall when I am tired from a long and hurried journey from London at your behest. As to my handwriting, you had a fair sample of it in my correspondence with you." Then she paused, smiled just a tiny, smug little smile and added, "I beg your pardon for my inaccuracy. My correspondence with your man, Nestor, I should have specified."

"Women!" his lordship snarled. But he did, finally, remember his manners and said grudgingly, "Very well, come into my study. We will talk this over sensibly, for you must see that it won't do for you to take the position. It won't do at all."

Alicia immediately unbuttoned her plain travelling pelisse and slid it from her shoulders. She handed it to the butler, who stood goggle-eyed at this insolence. As she began to untie her bonnet ribbons, his lordship protested vehemently, "You're not to stay, you know."

"Please make up your mind." Alicia was coolly polite. "You have invited me to discuss this contretemps with you. I choose to do it in comfort." She proceeded to hand the bonnet to the staid butler.

"Oh, very well, come along. Vernon, bring Madeira—unless Miss Fitzhugh prefers tea."

"A cup of tea would be most refreshing," she allowed.

The study was a masculine room, with heavy Kent furniture, and carpet and curtains in dark brown. There was a massive mahogany desk cluttered with sheets of foolscap. Pennsfield waved her to a seat, then chose to sit opposite her, with the desk between them.

On the edge of the desk nearest her, Alicia saw several books. Her keen eyes caught the titles and the author. All were novels by Lady D.

Raising her black eyebrows, Alicia leaned forward and picked up one of the books. "My lord, this seems scarcely the kind of book I'd expect you to enjoy. But then, I daresay they belong to Lady Pennsfield."

It was at once apparent that she had said the wrong thing.

Scowling darkly, he muttered, "There is no Lady Pennsfield."

"I beg your pardon. Then you like to read such trivial stuff?"

Immediately his back was up. "You have read some of Lady D's novels? If not, how can you comment on them?"

"I have one of them in my small valise. At times, when I am excessively weary, light and frivolous reading is to my liking. They scarcely are classics."

His face turned as dark as a summer thundercloud. "It is obvious that we don't deal together at all."

"Because I consider Lady D's novels light? Really, sir, I find this highly amusing."

"Lady D's novels sell in the thousands, Miss Fitzhugh."

"I never doubted that for a moment," she said. Whatever could ail the man? "Oh, I take it that Lady D is a friend of yours and I have offended you by my assessment of her books. I beg your pardon."

"Enough of this," he said, his voice as cold as a Scottish winter. "It is enough that we can never work well together."

Alicia looked him squarely in the eye and asked, "Because I don't think that Lady D's novels rank with Fielding or Richardson? Sir, my tastes in literature can have no bearing on my handwriting."

He said nothing, only lounged in his armchair and glared balefully at her.

Alicia began to worry. This encounter wasn't going at all well. It would be a terrible setback if this opinionated, supercilious man refused to allow her to stay here and work as a secretary. She'd have to go back to London and put up with the Season, with all the fortune hunters breathing heavily when they saw her. She had best make some effort to soothe his ruffled feathers.

"I fear we have started out on a wrong foot," she began pacifically. "I regret the ambiguity of my name. My mother's family are Welsh, hence Morgan."

"Women are deceitful by nature," he pronounced.

"I beg your pardon, sir." No matter that she'd planned to soothe his anger; Alicia St. John would never stand for such a slur on her character. "If there was any deceit, it was on your part. You tricked me, offering decent employment—and hiding behind your valet. I find that reprehensible."

It was the wrong thing to say, and she realized it the moment the words had left her lips. Darcy Cummings, Baron Pennsfield, let a slight, cold smile touch his handsome face. "Then, my dear Miss Fitzhugh, since you feel you have been grievously used, you will not wish to continue in my employ. I shall, of course, recompense you for your time."

"I refuse such a sop to my feelings," Alicia responded hotly. "I came here from London at your insistence, expecting gainful employ for a reasonable length of time." She looked pointedly at his splint-clad arm. "I assume you have broken a bone and cannot write for yourself."

"Even a ninnyhammer could assume that," he said ungraciously.

She glanced at his desk with a cool eye. "You seem to be in a state of confusion. Do you have so much correspondence that you need to hire a secretary? Couldn't someone here write your letters for you? Perhaps," she added slyly, "Mr. Nestor could do it. He seems to be quite adept at letter writing." She flaunted her letter of employment at Lord Pennsfield.

"You don't understand."

"Indeed, sir, I do not. Not having any Gypsy blood in my veins, I cannot read minds."

"I am an author," Lord Pennsfield finally said grudgingly.

She was so surprised that she allowed her astonishment to show on her face and widen her gray eyes. He gave a little smile of something that quite resembled triumph.

"Ah, Miss Morgan Fitzhugh, I have caught you off guard."

"Indeed you have, yet I might have guessed, seeing so much foolscap scattered about." Although his manner irked her, Alicia discovered that she was feeling some sympathy for this arrogant, opinionated fellow. "It must be difficult to have a broken arm when you are a writer. Did you fall?"

"Damned black brute of a stallion threw me," he snapped, "startled by a stoat that ran across the road under his nose."

"Pardon me for asking this, sir, but are you a published author? Or are you only hopeful?"

"I am a published author and I have a publisher who insists upon receiving my new novel by a certain date." He gestured awkwardly with his left hand. "Hence the need for a secretary."

"Then why send me away?" Alicia became sweet reasonableness. "I was hired to work as your secretary; I am here; I am quite capable of doing the work. If you choose to send me back to London, you must place another advertisement and lose even more time."

He glared at her, then said slowly and distinctly, as if she were a foreigner who understood little of the King's English, "I do not wish to work with a woman."

"There are times when we don't get our wishes. It seems to me that you have little choice. Place another advertisement, if you wish. In the meantime, you only spite yourself if you do not avail yourself of my assistance. I am here, ready to work."

She wasn't sure the ploy would work. He sat there, supporting his chin on his good hand, glaring at her as if she'd done something horrid to him. Very well, she had misled him by using only parts of her name; but he'd misled her, too. That made them even. Finally he nodded, a very grudging nod.

"Very well, Miss Fitzhugh, I have little choice. I will give you a trial. I trust you can write as I talk."

"I am sure I can. And now, what kind of novels do you write, sir?"

"You understand that I expect complete confidentiality?"

She nodded haughtily. "You can trust me completely."

He gave a bitter laugh. "I trust no woman. But at the moment, I am saddled with you. Very well." He smiled a wicked smile. "I shall tell you my secret." He reached across the desk and picked up one of the books. "I write under the pseudonym Lady D. I write these—what were the adjectives you used, Miss Fitzhugh—trivial? frivolous? light?—novels."

For once in her seven and twenty years, Lady Alicia felt at a loss for words. She sat still, her cheeks hot. Then she shook her head and said wryly, "I'm afraid I dug that pit for myself. Accept my apology, my lord. But then," she added, rallying, "I don't have to like what you write, do I? All I must do is transcribe it legibly."

Her words won a small smile from Lord Pennsfield.

"True, Miss Fitzhugh. Your function here is amanuensis, not critic."

A brief discussion of wages and terms of employment followed. The sum of money Lord Pennsfield mentioned was quite adequate—certainly far more than the paltry amounts Alicia had seen listed in the newspaper advertisements. He stressed that his need for her services would end as soon as his arm had healed. She agreed graciously to both the wage offered and the length of her employ.

There was a tap at the door, and Vernon brought in a tea tray, fragrant steam coming from the spout of the silver teapot.

"Ah, tea," Alicia said thankfully. "A truce, sir?"

He nodded, albeit reluctantly. "A truce, Miss Fitzhugh."

CHAPTER THREE

SURREPTITIOUSLY ALICIA massaged her aching fingers. She had been hard at work since early morning, discovering when a little maid brought in morning tea at the appalling hour of seven that his lordship always rose early and expected to be hard at work in the study as soon as he had breakfasted. Now it was mid-afternoon, and Alicia was so tired that she wanted nothing more than to go to her charming little bedchamber and sleep for hours.

Which room she should use had caused some problems last night. Once Lord Pennsfield had agreed that she might stay, he rang for Vernon. "We shall have to prepare a different bedchamber for Miss Fitzhugh." In exasperation he ran the long, slender fingers of his left hand through his silken pale hair.

"There is no need to make special arrangements for me," Alicia said quickly. "Any accommodation you have planned for a male secretary will be satisfactory for me."

"I scarcely think so," he said dryly. Then, to the butler, "The Rose Room, I think."

"Yes, milord."

As soon as Vernon had gone out, with his stately tread, Alicia objected, "Why make any special—"

"You are repeating yourself, Miss Fitzhugh. The room I planned to give my secretary connects with my own suite. At times I am restless at night and cannot sleep. When I could do my own scribbling, I often wrote at night. I had hoped I could prevail on my new man to help me at such odd hours—hence the convenience of having his bedchamber connecting with my own. Now you can see why you'll occupy the Rose Room."

"I see." He was so solemn about the whole affair that it was difficult not to laugh. "Is the Rose Room near your suite?" she asked, trying to keep her voice innocent of any innuendo.

"At the other end of the corridor," he said gruffly.

"I am here to be your secretary, sir. If you should wish to work at night, I am quite willing to do so. I was hired to help you, not hinder the creative muse. All you need do is call me, and I shall take your dictation no matter what the hour."

He'd looked at her suspiciously, then muttered, "We'll see." Truly he seemed to have an aversion to all women.

Now, her hand cramping from all the writing she'd done, her script so deteriorated that she wondered if she'd be able to read it when she made a fair copy, Alicia could only hope that his lordship didn't expect her to work all night. If he did, he'd not be the only one with his arm in a sling; for if she had to write many more lines of this revolting prose, her hand might drop off.

Just then Pennsfield stopped dictating and stretched like a huge cat. "Be a good fellow—lady—and ring for tea. You're closer to the bellpull than I."

Glad to do anything that wasn't writing, Alicia laid aside her pen and walked to the embroidered tapestry bellpull.

"Tired, Miss Fitzhugh?"

Seeing a spark of mischief in his blue eyes, she said dryly, "Tired? Except for my hand, which may fall off onto this lovely Turkey carpet, and my shoulders, which ache to my toes, I am not at all tired, sir."

He gave her a keen, knowing look. "You have worked a long time as a secretary, Miss Fitzhugh?"

Ah, he was suspicious already. "My work has been more in the line of social correspondence—addressing invitation cards, answering notes, you know the kind of thing. You are the first author for whom I've worked." There, she'd not quite lied to him; but Alicia realized that even though he wrote nonsense, Darcy Cummings was no feathertop. He had a keen mind, and she'd have to be on her toes constantly to keep him from finding out her secret. Having already seen his temper displayed, she was not anxious to have it vented on her. If he found out how he'd been tricked, heaven help her.

She was beginning to wonder, though, how she was to meet the man of her dreams while hidden away here at Pennsfield Manor. Perhaps she had been hasty in her choice of situations. She could always resign it; but she couldn't leave immediately. His accident had caused Pennsfield to fall woefully behind with his new novel, and he had to have it finished by the date his publisher had fixed on. She'd not feel right to leave him in the lurch before the work was ready to post off to the publisher.

"I think we've done enough for one day," Pennsfield said as they sat in the study sipping tea. "I trust you will join me for dinner."

Alicia had wondered what arrangement he'd make about meals. Was she to eat with the servants in the kitchen? Breakfast had been served on a tray in her bedchamber, and they'd both lunched from trays here in the study.

"I shall be happy to dine with you."

Alicia sensed that Lord Pennsfield was a lonely man, drawn in on himself. Had there been some tragedy in his life, or some disastrous affair of the heart? He'd been so vehement in his remarks about women last evening. However, they had dealt quite well together today, perhaps because she was able to keep up with his dictation, although it hadn't been easy. After dinner, if she could hold a pen, she must make a fair copy of what she'd scrawled in haste during the day. If she waited too long, she might never be able to decipher it. Also, she meant to make some slight changes in a few places; some infelicitous phrasing could be improved. Surely that was one function of a good secretary.

She didn't need too much time to decide on which gown to wear to dinner. She had pared her wardrobe to the bone, leaving all of her finer things in Berkeley Square. She would wear the British net frock over a blue satin slip. It was cut quite low over the bosom; but her bosom was one to display. The waist of the gown was very short, just under the bustline, and the sleeves were short and decorated with knots of blue ribbon. The skirt was quite full and was finished at the hem with a narrow rouleau of satin. She considered wearing a Kent toque of bright yellow Parisian gauze, but decided that it was too dressy for a simple dinner with her employer. She also decided against her sapphire necklace and earrings. She should never have brought good jewelry with her. No secretary would own such fine pieces as these.

When she descended the circular staircase, Vernon was just ushering into the house a tall, sturdy young man dressed in the latest fashion, his blue *frac* fitting like a second skin. His dark hair and eyes gave him a Gypsy look. Hearing her footsteps on the stairs, he looked up, and his eyes widened with surprise. Then he made a polite bow before walking over to meet her as she descended.

"What astounding good fortune," he said in a deep, mellow baritone. "I had no idea that Darcy was entertaining such a charmer. May I present myself, as my host seems not to be down yet? I am Sir Hilary Ingham, Darcy's nearest and dearest neighbor. My estate is Ravenswood."

Alicia knew that predatory look and immediately pegged Sir Hilary as another fortune hunter. Then she remembered that he didn't know she was an heiress. Smiling prettily, she dropped a curtsy and said, "I'm Miss Morgan Fitzhugh."

"What a charming name—Morgan," he burbled. "Shall we wait for Darcy in the drawing room?" He offered his arm and escorted her toward paneled doors leading into a pretty white-and-blue room she'd not seen before. Vernon opened the doors for them, murmuring that he'd tell his lordship Sir Hilary had arrived.

"Unexpectedly," Sir Hilary said jocularly. "Always get a good meal here at Pennsfield Manor. Darcy sets a good table."

Vernon poured Madeira for them, then went off to inform his master that he had a guest.

"And where has Darcy been hiding you, Miss Fitzhugh?" the bluff gentleman asked, eyeing her hungrily. "He's been such a recluse this past year. I'm glad to see he's recovered."

Not having any idea what Sir Hilary was talking about, Alicia only opened her fan and hid behind it. Had Lord Pennsfield been ill? Maybe that explained his brusque manner.

At that moment he entered the room, the severe black and white of his evening dress a perfect match for his blond elegance. "Hilary, I wasn't expecting you. Have you met Miss Fitzhugh?"

"Indeed I have, and I am green with envy. Wherever did you find a lady of quality to grace Pennsfield Manor?"

Quickly, to allay further misunderstanding, Alicia struck in with, "I am his lordship's secretary, Sir Hilary."

"His what?"

Pennsfield, who had seemed more genial when he came in to them, stiffened up at this and snapped, "Is your hearing impaired? You heard Miss Fitzhugh.

With my broken wing, I need someone to help me with my . . . correspondence.''

Alicia noticed the tiny hesitation, but apparently Sir Hilary didn't.

"I don't believe any of this nonsense," he declared. "You're gammoning me, both of you. I know quality when I see it; and you, Miss Fitzhugh, are quality."

"Thank you, sir," she murmured, but she was quick to see that Lord Pennsfield was annoyed by Sir Hilary's words.

"I'm afraid your special sense has left you this time, Hilary." He turned to Alicia, a tinge of malice in his voice. "Hilary thinks he has unerring perception when a fortune is in the room."

"I don't understand." But Alicia did understand, of course. She'd been subjected to this kind of man since her come-out when she was seventeen. Sir Hilary must be poor. Such men developed an uncanny nose for the blunt, sniffing out heiresses as cleverly as a hound sniffs out a fox.

"Pay our host no heed, Miss Morgan—if I may be so bold as to call you that. It is a charming name, so unusual."

"His lordship found it highly unusual," Alicia said, a sly smile on her face.

Pennsfield winced but recovered himself.

"Well, I shan't have to warn Miss Fitzhugh about you, Hilary, now that you know she's not a woman of means."

Sir Hilary, frowning, gave Alicia a most penetrating look. "I cannot understand," he muttered. "She has all of the attributes...

"I'd scarcely have traveled all the way from London to work as his lordship's secretary if I were an heiress," she said quietly.

"I stand corrected." But clearly Sir Hilary wasn't convinced. Then he turned to Lord Pennsfield, saying heartily, "At least you are coming out of your shell if you've hired such a charmer as Miss Morgan to lighten your days."

"I've hired her merely to wield the pen I can't hold. Come along, Vernon must be ready to serve."

As if on command, the butler came to the drawing room door to announce that dinner was served.

Sir Hilary kept up a steady stream of chatter through the meal, although Alicia noticed that it didn't stop him from eating heartily, devouring woodcock, roast mutton and a whole young chicken, along with a variety of vegetables. She and their host dined more lightly.

"Always sure of a fine meal here, Darcy," Sir Hilary said, "but I'd scarcely expected such delicious dessert," and he raised his wineglass to Alicia. "To you, Miss Morgan."

She nodded graciously.

While they waited for the footman to clear the main course, Alicia asked, to keep intelligent conversation going, "And what do you think of our new regent?"

"Parliament had little choice, I suppose," Sir Hilary said. "King George is mad."

"Oh, I'm not sure of that," Alicia objected. "He's old and ill, that I'll concede; but mad?"

"Well, the Prince had his work cut out for him with the Whigs and the Tories at each other's throats. What do you think of having a regent, Darcy?"

"I don't concern myself with politics." Pennsfield had lapsed into silence as dinner progressed.

"But you should," Alicia protested. "Private citizens get the kind of government they deserve. All of us should be informed and make our voices heard."

"Good God! A bluestocking," he muttered ungraciously.

"Scarcely that," she retorted tartly. "But a woman doesn't have to simper and say 'whatever you say, sir' to every remark a man utters. Surely you men must find that boring."

He took up her challenge. "Affairs of state are men's business, my dear Miss Fitzhugh. Men prefer women who have more feminine concerns and less . . . belligerent views."

"What fustian! Do you honestly expect me to believe that you enjoy the company of vapid little beauties who have nothing in their feathertops except thought of the next party, the next flirtation, the next male conquest? Truly, you know little of women if you think we are all of that ilk."

She realized she'd probably overstepped the line, but male condescension was more than she could bear.

"Hear, hear!" Sir Hilary laughed uproariously and lifted his glass in a silent toast to her. Then he added, a sly look on his florid face, "Miss Morgan is a far cry from Lady Beatrice, isn't she, Darcy?"

There was a sudden stillness that almost frightened Alicia. She saw a look of guilt flit over Sir Hilary's face, as if he knew he'd gone much too far.

Lord Pennsfield looked as if he might explode. His blue eyes crackled with rage as he said slowly and distinctly, as if to a backward child, "Don't ever mention that name in my presence again, Ingham, or you'll find your welcome here has evaporated like morning mist once the sun burns down on it. Do you understand me, Ingham?"

Thoroughly abashed, Sir Hilary nodded and murmured an apology. In a few minutes, he begged to be excused, pleading an early start next day since he had promised to ride over his estate with his bailiff.

Under the circumstances, Alicia felt it best to go to her own bedchamber, although she normally would have enjoyed further conversation. Pennsfield barely nodded to her when she bade him good night.

Once in her own room, she thought about copying the day's work, but as her hand still ached from holding a pen all day, she decided to have an early night and do her copying before breakfast. She would still be able to make out her hasty scrawl in the morning.

Tired as she was, though, she had trouble in falling asleep. Who was Lady Beatrice? There was some mystery connected with this name, and she didn't know how to ferret out the solution. She could scarcely quiz the servants, although they probably would gossip to her if given half a chance. Still, she was in a rather unenviable position here, neither fish nor fowl, not a servant in the usual sense of the word, yet an employee. If only she could get a chance to chat with Sir Hilary, she might extract from him the story of Lady Beatrice. However, after the terrible setdown given him by Lord Pennsfield, Alicia thought she would not see her neighbor from Ravenswood at Pennsfield Manor soon.

Tomorrow, if she had time and wasn't too tired, she'd write to Hon Zella to find out if she'd heard any *on-dits* about her handsome employer. He was an exasperating fellow. If that simpleton Ingham hadn't ruined everything with his remark about the mysterious Lady Beatrice, Alicia would have taken him to task for his cut at women with unfeminine concerns and belligerent views. It was obvious that his words were aimed at her; yet he had accepted her as a secretary, albeit unwillingly. If she was as silly as he seemed to want women to be, she would not be able to do her job with any proficiency. No, Lord Pennsfield really needed a setdown. If he gave her another such opening, she'd scorch his ears.

With this satisfying thought, she fell asleep, only to dream of a mysterious veiled woman named Beatrice.

CHAPTER FOUR

LADY ALICIA GROANED softly when Fanny waked her by drawing the curtains and letting in the morning sunshine. She had already placed Alicia's tea tray on a walnut stand by her bed. Seeing that the new secretary was awake, Fanny asked, "Do you wish for hot water now, miss, or will you drink tea first?"

Alicia propped herself up on her pillows and untied her lawn nightcap. Yawning hugely, she said, "Tea first, or I shall not survive." Rising at this unholy hour was one part of her masquerade she'd not expected, nor did she relish it. Alicia was accustomed to late nights in London, with balls and parties going on until all hours. She rarely rose before eleven.

Fanny brought her a damp cloth to wipe her face, then handed her a soft, fluffy towel.

"There's a note from his lordship on your tea tray, miss."

Now what? Alicia wondered, contemplating the almost illegible scrawl on the folded paper.

Fanny giggled. "Looks like hen scratching, don't it, Miss Fitzhugh? He had to write it with his left hand."

With some difficulty, Alicia managed to decipher the note, which told her that Lord Pennsfield was driving out to Bakewell, and would return by noon.

She was to prepare a fair copy of yesterday's dictation while she waited.

"His lordship often rode in the morning before he broke his arm," Fanny volunteered as she poured another cup of steaming tea for Alicia. Obviously the little maid, brown eyes sparkling beneath a snowy mobcap, wanted to gossip. "Now he usually has Odbert drive him in his phaeton. I think it irks him a lot, miss. Sometimes, you know, he gets terrible black moods and used to be able to ride to get rid of them." The saucy maid glanced around as if she expected her master to be hiding behind the carved walnut wardrobe. Then, leaning toward Alicia, she murmured, "It's all since he was left waiting at the church, you know."

Aha! Alicia saw a glimmering of truth. Although at home she never encouraged Sally, her maid, to gossip, she needed information to maintain her position at Pennsfield Manor. Perhaps Fanny could help her ferret out the reason for Lord Pennsfield's aversion to women. She didn't ask anything, but she opened her gray eyes just a bit wider and waited, sure the maid would rattle away.

"It was Lady Beatrice Underhill, Miss Fitzhugh. Oh, she was the talk of Derbyshire, she was."

"A lady?" Alicia filled her voice with skepticism, hoping that it would bring on more explanation.

"Would you care for toast and marmalade, miss?" Fanny lifted silver covers to reveal an appetizing breakfast. "She's a lady in her own right, and she was living at Foxmere on the other side of the county. Tiny, blond and very lively. Very lively indeed, miss, if you take my meaning." This was all delivered in a conspiratorial tone, with much guilty glancing around, as if there might be eavesdroppers hiding behind the curtains or under the four-poster.

Alicia, now thoroughly awake, had difficulty keeping a straight face. "Do you mean she was . . . fast?" Immediately she was sorry for leading this little servant on.

"Well, miss, it's not for me to talk about my betters," Fanny said, "but everyone in the servants' hall was shocked when we heard his lordship was going to marry her. Of course," she added ingenuously, "Lady Beatrice has a considerable fortune."

Alicia let her eyes take in the lovely appointments of the room, and thought of the elegance of the main salons on the ground floor, where the rugs were Turkish, the silver all heavy, the china Minton. "I'd scarcely think Lord Pennsfield needs to marry a woman with a fortune," she probed. "He can't be short of the blunt."

"But you know how it is with the nobility," Fanny said, putting Lady Alicia squarely in the servants' corner, "they never can have too much money. Money marries money."

"Often fortune hunters marry money," Alicia answered caustically.

"Well, his lordship certainly isn't that," Fanny said, as if she'd been personally insulted.

"No, no, I didn't mean that for a moment. Of course, he does seem a bit tetchy, and I don't think he's overfond of women. . . ." She didn't want Fanny to stop her story now.

"No wonder, miss, as Lady Beatrice treated him so badly." She shook her head, little brown ringlets bouncing under the ruffle of her cap. "Can you imagine any woman who'd turn down Lord Pennsfield for someone else?"

As Lady Alicia found her employer arrogant and uncivil, she could think of lots of women who would not care to share his title, herself among them. She made a little noncommittal, encouraging sound.

"He was already at St. George's, waiting for her to arrive for the wedding. The church was crowded with nobs from everywhere, even up from London. Then this little urchin came in."

"You were there?"

"Indeed I was, miss. Vernon gave us all time off. We worked like navvies, up at four, to get everything ready for welcoming our new mistress, just so's we could see his lordship married. This little lad comes in, all tatters, and when they tried to shoo him out, he says he has a message for the groom. Marched right up the aisle, bold as brass, with a note in his hand. His lordship read it, then turned black as a thundercloud. He crumpled the note into a wad, flung it down and strode out of the church without a word to anyone, even the rector. He took the first horse he happened on—the Earl of Fanshaw's prize mare—and galloped off. He turned up here next day, somewhat the worse for drink."

"And what of Lady Beatrice?" Alicia couldn't keep herself from asking.

Fanny giggled. "Ran off with her gamekeeper, she did. Edward Lambert. Handsome enough—oh, he was one for the ladies, he was!"

Lady Alicia's eyes popped wide from real shock. "Her ladyship married her gamekeeper!"

"Well, miss, no one knows for sure. They might have ridden to Scotland and pledged over the anvil. Many think she didn't bother with any wedding ceremony. No one's seen hide nor hair of her since that day."

Alicia was torn: after such treatment no wonder her employer disliked women, yet he was so boorish to her that she had some difficulty in feeling suitably sympathetic.

"How do the servants feel about this?"

"Well, miss, his lordship is really a very good master. I know he gets his temper up and shouts at us sometimes; but Pennsfield Manor is a good place to be in service, believe me."

Alicia's jet eyebrows rose at this. No doubt little Fanny had a *tendresse* for her master, a common enough occurrence. Fleetingly she wondered if Pennsfield dallied with the servants. The impression of him she had gotten was not that of a man who seduced his maids.

Now she must rise, wash and dress. Her work waited for her. By the time Alicia had copied Pennsfield's dictation from yesterday, her hands ached again. She'd heard of writer's cramp. Now she knew what it was. She had changed a few things, improving on his wording. In a place or two, Alicia had toned down what she considered purple prose. "Eyes like deep pools in which Sir Mallory longed to swim,'' was a bit too strong for her stomach.

The pretty ormolu clock on her chimneypiece was just striking eleven when Alicia finished her copying. Stretching to ease the ache in her shoulders, she rose and went to the window, which looked down on part of the carefully laid out gardens surrounding Pennsfield Manor. She saw the clever hand of Capability Brown in the design, for a lovely vista showed, artfully contrived to seem as though the lawns and trees had grown to make the prospect without man's help. Perhaps she'd stroll in the gardens until luncheon. She should write to Hon Zella; but her hands ached at the thought of picking up the pen again. Perhaps she should have chosen some slightly less tiring occupation. Alicia had always been an enthusiastic letter writer with a huge correspondence. It had not occurred to her that secretarial writing would be so different and so strenuous. She'd not mention this to Hon Zella, for that clever lady would only nod and say, "I told you so, Alicia."

Slipping on a rather plain green velvet spencer and tying on her bonnet, Alicia hurried down the magnificent curving staircase to the great hall, then went out a side door to the garden she'd been admiring. It was nice to be in the open air, and she strolled about, appreciating the work of the gardeners, until she began to feel hungry. Glancing at the dainty gold watch pinned to her spencer, Alicia saw that it was time for the noon meal. She turned and walked quickly back, only to be stopped in her tracks by an angry bellow from the house.

"Miss Fitzhugh! Where are you?"

She recognized the not-so-dulcet tones of her employer, obviously back from his ride. Although he himself had set noon as the time he would return, Alicia was chagrined that she had not been available when he was ready to start work. Picking up her skirts, she hurried along the gravel path toward the tall glass doors leading from his lordship's study onto the flagged terrace.

Like some avenging spirit, Lord Pennsfield stood in the open doorway, some sheets of foolscap clutched in his left hand.

Breathless from hurrying, she scurried across the terrace to confront him, wondering what new crisis had enraged him—for every line of his body was a clear delineation of anger.

"I'm sorry to keep you waiting, my lord," she gasped, only to have the sheaf of pages shaken under her nose.

"I thought you were an experienced secretary," he shouted, the cords in his neck, not completely hidden by his collar and carelessly folded neckcloth, standing out like ropes. "You have taken liberties with my prose, Miss Fitzhugh. I won't have it, do you hear?"

"Indeed I do hear, and no doubt everyone for miles around can hear also. There is no need to shout at me. I am not deaf."

His blue eyes were dark with fury. Alicia was not used to being addressed in such a tone of voice and she resented it profoundly.

"And insolent, too. I knew it wouldn't work. I didn't want a woman mangling my prose."

Her own Irish temper now began steaming. A few more statements such as those and it would come to a full rolling boil. "You prefer to have a man mangle your prose, sir?"

"Don't be insolent with me, Miss Fitzhugh. Did you think I'd not notice the changes you made in my manuscript?"

"Oh, those," she said, relaxing. "Heavens, I thought I'd done something terrible, considering the fuss you're making."

First he flushed, then he turned chalky white. Was he going to have apoplexy? He stepped aside, motioned her into his study. "Sit down, Miss Fitzhugh. I have a few words I want you to hear."

She sat reluctantly, knowing it put her at a disadvantage, for now he towered over her like some avenging spirit.

"I am the author," he said, voice now silkily deadly. "You—" he pointed at her dramatically "—are the secretary."

Goaded by the accusing finger, Alicia allowed her temper to rise to meet his. "I am aware of those simple facts. I even understand them, although I'm but a lowly woman, while you are a lordly man, clever enough to allow himself to be thrown from his horse."

"How dare you!"

"I'm not accustomed to being shouted at, Lord Pennsfield." If he'd known Alicia better, he'd have been warned when her warm gray eyes turned a cold slate color.

"I'm not accustomed to having a secretary who takes on herself the job of altering my manuscript."

Alicia shrugged. "You're not accustomed to having a secretary of any sort, sir. And I must add, in all truth, that if you dismiss me, you'll have trouble finding another who'll put up with your tantrums."

"Tantrums!" he yelled, shaking the sheaf of manuscript pages so hard that Alicia knew they'd be crumpled in a minute. Having risen betimes to make a fair copy of yesterday's dictation, she couldn't bear to watch her work being ruined, so she stood up, forcing Pennsfield to step back, and plucked the pages from his fingers. Then she made a show of smoothing them.

"Now see what you've done," she chided, "when I worked so hard to make a neat copy for you."

"I can't see that it matters, Miss Fitzhugh, as you'll have to transcribe my dictation again."

"Why, pray? I thought you were in such a rush to finish this novel according to your timetable."

"My novel—not yours, Miss Fitzhugh."

"Oh, really, my lord, what a tempest in a teapot," Alicia scolded, frowning at him. Grown men had been known to quake at her famous frown. "I changed a only a few places where the prose was execrable."

"Execrable! I am so glad to hear your opinion of my writing." His tone was equally quelling. "My readers do not agree with you. My books sell remarkably well."

"I daresay. Even I have bought them on occasion—when I wanted some fluffy concoction to chase away boredom."

Now he stamped about the study, not quite frothing at the mouth. "I will not tolerate such insolence!"

Tired of all this acrimony and annoyed with herself for having launched her harebrained scheme at all, Alicia faced her irate employer.

"Very well, sir, you have my resignation. I shall now go to my room, pack and leave. Of course you'll lose at least a week while you place another advertisement—but that is no concern of mine."

She turned and marched to the study door. Her hand was on the knob when Pennsfield said, "Not so fast, Miss Spitfire. You agreed to work for me, and work you shall. I am all too aware of the minutes fleeing." In a tone intended to be mollifying, he added, "I must say you do write a fine hand."

Alicia knew it galled him to have to ask her to remain and she was fair enough to know she owed him another chance. Without her he would never finish the book in time. But she didn't intend to knuckle under to his bad temper. He needed taking down a peg, did Darcy Cummings, Baron Pennsfield, and she might just be the one to do it.

"Very well, my lord, I shall stay, at least until you can find a suitable replacement for me. But I think it might be wise for you to write to the *Gazette* today to place your advertisement. Now, sir," she went on briskly, "about those changes. In just a few places where your prose became...excessive, I only toned it down, made it slightly less florid, a bit more palatable."

"Palatable to whom? Those who read my novels like my style."

To prove her point, Alicia leafed through the copy she'd made. "Oh, Gwendolyn, light of my life, if you will not accept my heart, then I shall throw myself into the black depths of yon lake and die." Her mouth curled into a moue of rejection. "Do you think people talk this way?"

"Of course not, you ninnyhammer," he exploded. "This is fiction, not biography. People read novels to be taken out of themselves, to forget the day-to-day humdrum of their lives, to find romance."

She sighed loudly. "Can't they be romantic while talking with a little more sense?"

Voice dangerously low, Pennsfield said, "I think I want to start dictating now, Miss Fitzhugh. Take a letter."

Quickly she sat down at the small desk he had provided for her use and dipped her pen into the German crystal inkwell set in a silver base. "I am ready."

"Address it to the *Gazette* in London. Gentlemen, I wish to place an advertisement in your newspaper. I require a secretary."

Alicia knew she'd invited this setdown. She had provoked his lordship more than was reasonable on her part; and she had offered to resign. Nevertheless, much to her surprise, she discovered that this letter wasn't to her liking. Although she and Pennsfield didn't deal at all well together, and though she resented being called a ninnyhammer, still it was a defeat to find he intended to replace her at the first opportunity. Now she'd have to start again. Remembering most of the positions advertised in the *Ga-zette*, she realized that this was the only one that had sounded even faintly interesting.

Was she going to have to go back to London and endure the vapid young men who would dangle after her because she had a fortune? Even his lordship looked a prize compared to them.

CHAPTER FIVE

LADY ALICIA LOOKED at her reflection in the long, gilt-framed mirror, wondering if her gown was too elaborate for her supposed station in life. It had been difficult for her to prepare a suitable wardrobe in the short time she had had before journeying to Derbyshire. She lifted one side of the thin jaconet muslin round dress to make sure that the peach-colored sarcenet slip was falling gracefully from the high waist. Except for a fall of lace at the throat, the gown was rather plain. She hoped it was a proper gown for a secretary to wear to tea. She and Pennsfield were to take tea with his mother, Jocelyn, the dowager Lady Pennsfield, who lived in the Dower House at the end of the formal garden behind Pennsfield Manor.

She pulled on a spencer of white striped lutestring with braid trimming on the front. She hadn't brought many bonnets, deciding that she mustn't appear affluent, but she had not been able to resist a large leghorn hat trimmed with peach satin dyed to match the slip.

As she picked up a beaded reticule, there was a tap at her bedchamber door, and Fanny came in to tell her that his lordship was waiting in the phaeton. "Although how he plans to drive one-handed, I don't know, miss," she added.

Alicia's eyebrows rose precipitously. "A phaeton just to go to the other end of the garden? How droll. I had assumed we would walk there."

"Oh, no, miss, his lordship never walks. Until he broke his arm, he rode. Now he's limited to carriages. I think," Fanny added confidentially, "he's taking the phaeton just to prove he can drive with one hand."

"Well, if it develops that he has overestimated his ability as a whip, I can take the ribbons," Alicia declared, pulling on fine Irish leather gloves.

"He'd never allow a woman to drive for him, miss, begging your pardon, of course."

"It's all right, Fanny. I know his opinion of women," was her rueful reply.

Alicia had written out the note to the *Gazette*, but she didn't think Pennsfield had mailed it yet. Secretly she was pleased. She was a little ashamed to think she'd allowed her temper to show and earn her dismissal. For several days she had scrupulously copied his dictation verbatim, although some of his prose was still so overblown that it set her teeth on edge. Ah, well, she didn't have to buy more of his romances.

She wondered how many here at Pennsfield Manor knew he was the author known as Lady D. She'd not heard a breath on the subject from Fanny, who was an inveterate gossip. This was surprising. Most servants knew all of the master's secrets. Probably the valet, Nestor, knew; but he'd guard the secret jealously.

It was a lovely day, and Alicia wished she could have the phaeton to herself, for she loved to drive. Fanny's words precluded any chance of that.

The phaeton was a highflyer, and the matched roans attached to it were some of the finest horseflesh she'd seen.

"Come along, come along, Miss Fitzhugh," his lordship called impatiently. "These cattle are high-strung. They don't like standing."

A footman handed her up to the high seat, and the moment she'd settled herself, Pennsfield shook the ribbons and the team pranced around the circular drive.

"I don't suppose you'd like me to drive," she asked, noticing how awkward it was for him to handle ribbons and whip one-handed.

"You suppose correctly, Miss Fitzhugh. I've never seen a good woman driver yet."

Miffed, she said, "I am a good whip. Better than many men I know who think they are nonpareils."

"Indeed. Modesty is not one of your attributes, is it? You alter my writing, now you hint you handle the ribbons better than I."

"I didn't say that, sir—but I do have two usable hands."

"That is a low blow, Miss Fitzhugh," he said, blue eyes cold as a winter's sky. "But where did you learn to drive? Have you ever driven those kind ladies who recommended you?"

Alicia couldn't resist this opening. Demurely she replied, "I have frequently driven Lady Alicia St. John."

"And did she find you proficient?"

"She never once complained." She wished she could prolong this delicious conversation, but unfortunately they had arrived at the Dower House, a charming cottage, two stories of local stone, with a handsome dormered roof.

A young lad hurried out to take the team, while his lordship sprang down from the high seat and helped Alicia with his good hand. She noticed that he glanced quickly at the short display of ankle he was afforded. It gave her surprising pleasure to have attracted such attention.

As they walked toward the door of his mother's house, Pennsfield murmured, "I must warn you, Miss Fitzhugh, not to let slip anything about my writing. If my mother should inquire, I have hired you to help me with my extensive correspondence."

"She does not know you are a published author?"

"No. And I prefer that she not learn it."

"You hired me to keep your secret, Lord Pennsfield. I shall not play you false."

The door was opened by a middle-aged woman whose gray hair was pulled back in an uncompromising fashion and held in place with a lace cap. Her gown was gray, with touches of snowy lawn at neck and cuff. She dropped a perfunctory curtsy and said in a no-nonsense voice, "Her ladyship is expecting you and Miss Fitzhugh, milord. She has another guest."

"Oh, bother. Who is it, Etta?"

"A lady author, milord."

"Good God!" Pennsfield muttered so that only Alicia could hear him. "Very well, Etta, lead us to the slaughter."

"She's quite a pleasant young woman, the authoress," Etta said severely, with the liberty of a trusted family servant.

"Very well, I stand corrected. We shall wallow in reflected glory, shall we not, Miss Fitzhugh?"

Alicia, who was having difficulty keeping a straight face, only smiled at him. Another author. What great fun this should be!

Etta ushered them into a charming salon decorated in the Adam style, with elegant Chippendale furnishings. An imperious lady sat in an armchair, her feet on a footstool. Beside her sat the woman Alicia had met briefly at the Rutland Arms, Miss Jane Austen. So she was an authoress! Remembering the woman's sensible manner, Alicia was sure she did not stoop to writing the sort of nonsense Lord Pennsfield daily dictated to her.

After the introductions were made and Alicia and her employer seated, Etta brought in the tea, which the dowager baroness poured.

"I was anxious that you should make the acquaintance of Miss Austen," the dowager told them. "She is staying here in the Peak District for the summer, revising a most delightful novel, which I have been privileged to see in part."

"Have you been published, Miss Austen?" Pennsfield asked in a rather supercilious tone. "I do not recall seeing books with your name on them."

In her gentle voice, Miss Austen said, "My first published work will be brought out later this year, sir, but my name will not be on it. I wish to remain anonymous."

"And the title?" Alicia asked. "I shall be eager to obtain a copy when it is published."

"I have called it *Sense and Sensibility*."

"And we all wish her good fortune and much success," Lady Pennsfield said firmly. "Having read parts of her new novel, I can assure you that her writing is elegant and witty, never running into the dreadful prose imposed on the public by such as Lady D."

Alicia, who was just taking a sip of tea, nearly choked when she heard these words. She peeped over the rim of her cup at Lord Pennsfield, amused to see him bristle.

His mother went on, quite unconscious of the effect her words were having. "Obviously Lady D is no lady!"

"You've read her works, Mama?"

"Someone gave me one of her novels, which I was quite unable to finish. Such overblown phrases! Such lurid situations! Oh, well, such trash has its admirers, no doubt." She turned to Alicia. "Have you read any of Lady D's works, Miss Fitzhugh?"

"I must admit, ma'am, that I have on occasion picked one up when I am tired or disheartened and need something light to read."

Disapproval on her patrician face, her ladyship recommended, "You would do better to read Richardson or Fielding." Remembering the bawdy nature of some of Fielding's novels, Alicia was secretly amused. She did agree, though, that they ranked as literature, while Pennsfield's work was drivel.

Incensed at the attack on his books, his lordship looked at Miss Austen and asked belligerently, "And are your novels destined to be read by generations to come, Miss Austen? Are they on noble themes?"

With a sweet smile, she replied, "Indeed no, sir. I have penned them only for my own amusement and for the enjoyment of my relations. It was they who urged me to publish them. As to weighty themes, mine are only stories of ordinary people."

"Ah, but you have such insight into their characters, Miss Austen," Lady Pennsfield insisted. "Your observations are both profound and witty, a most felicitous combination in any author. I predict great success for Miss Austen."

"Then I wish you good fortune."

Alicia suspected he resented having to say these polite words. Poor man, to be treated to such a diatribe by his own mother. She wondered what her ladyship would say if she knew the truth. A scene between mother and son when she learned the identity of Lady D would make interesting listening.

"By the most amusing coincidence, Darcy, Miss Austen's new hero shares your name."

At those words, Alicia saw something akin to alarm flit over the lady's face momentarily before she composed her features.

"It is true I had chosen to call him Mr. Darcy," she said quietly, "but if that should be an embarrassment to you, sir, I shall change it."

"No, no, I wouldn't want you to change your novel to accommodate me."

Alicia added one little gibe. "Perhaps you will achieve fame through reflected glory when Miss Austen's next novel is published."

If looks could kill, she'd have died on the spot.

Lady Pennsfield, unaware of all these crosscurrents, went on with her discussion of her guest's work. "This new novel has a charming theme, Darcy. A young woman in rather ordinary circumstances falls in love with a wealthy man who loves her but cannot stand her family, particularly her silly mama."

"And what is the result of such an unlikely union?" Lord Pennsfield asked.

Miss Austen smiled mischievously. "As you know, all love stories must have a happy ending."

"In that case, he doesn't marry the girl," Darcy replied.

Alicia was irate that her employer should so insult one as genuinely intelligent as Miss Austen; but she held her tongue. It wasn't her place to apologize for his bad manners.

His mother, though, had no such compunction. "Now, now, Darcy, that's not quite the thing. Just because you have had a distressing disappointment with a young woman, you should not think that love is going to go out of style."

Alicia thought that Lady Pennsfield had great strength of character to chide her son so pointedly. No doubt he took after his mother.

Although he scowled blackly, he had the grace to say, "I beg your pardon, Miss Austen. It is not for me to criticize your story, not having read it."

"No apology is necessary," she said with a little smile. "Tastes in literature differ. There's certainly room in England for both Lady D and me."

As if finally aware of the tensions in her salon, the dowager turned to Alicia to draw her into the conversation. "Darcy tells me you are helping with his correspondence while his arm heals. I offered to write for him, but he thought his mail too voluminous for me to deal with. I cannot imagine his having so many letters to write that he needs a secretary."

Before Alicia had to make some answer, Pennsfield cut in smoothly. "She also helps with the estate books, Mama. There's a great deal of work to running Pennsfield Manor."

"Not that I am ungrateful to you, Miss Fitzhugh," his mother continued. "I am glad to see my son taking a more active interest in his social life again. He mentioned your letters of recommendation, Miss Fitzhugh. I was delighted to see that one of them is from an old friend of mine."

Alicia felt incipient panic, but forced herself to remain calm. "Indeed, ma'am, how interesting."

"I went to Miss Quail's school with Gisella Montague when we were young. Alas, I have lost touch with her. I am glad to learn of her whereabouts and shall pen a missive to her soon, renewing old acquaintance. She never married?"

"No. Her betrothed died of a fever."

"Harry, wasn't that his name? I do remember now hearing something about it. But it was such a long time ago."

Alicia knew she'd have to write immediately to Hon Zella to warn her about the dowager. Bother! Was there no spot in England remote enough to contain her secret?

Lady Pennsfield rang for more tea. As she poured it for her guests, a knock was heard and Etta left the room to answer it. She returned almost immediately, lips thinned to a harsh line, carrying a tray with a calling card on it as if the card might explode.

Lady Pennsfield picked up the card, peered at it through a quizzing glass, then said quietly, "I am not at home, Etta."

There was a flash of triumph on that austere face, and the servant walked with quick little steps from the salon.

Pennsfield raised pale eyebrows and asked, "Someone you choose not to receive, Mama?"

"Exactly. Someone who is not quite the thing, Darcy."

His lordship just grinned as if accustomed to his mother's moods, then held out his cup for more tea.

Alicia, truly interested in Miss Austen's writing, asked, "Are you from this area, Miss Austen?"

"No, I'm living in Chawton now. I felt I needed solitude for another revision of my book. Now that I'm here, I have found the area so delightful that I shall use it in my novel, suitably disguised, of course." Then, eagerly, "Have you been to Chatsworth yet, Miss Fitzhugh?"

"No, although I understand it is magnificent."

"I intend to pattern my hero's home after the house," Miss Austen confided.

"I shall arrange for both of you to attend some social function there," the dowager promised. "I am on good terms with the Duchess of Devonshire."

"Will I be included, too, dear Lady Pennsfield?"

The interruption was electrifying, four heads turning to the door as if pulled by a puppeteer's strings. Standing there was a beautiful woman of about Alicia's age, certainly not just out of the schoolroom. She was small and shapely, a fact revealed by her modish riding habit, which was cut in the style known as *Amazone en Drap*. The jacket was very short, with tiny flared skirts, and it fitted her ample bosom admirably. The long side of the skirt was looped up to a fastening at the high waist. Her hat was a modified high hat in a scarlet felt that matched the color of the habit exactly. A light veil was draped fetchingly about the crown and flowed down at one side.

Eyes as bright and hard as amethysts glittered under perfectly arched brows, which were darker than the golden hair peeping out from under the brim of the riding hat.

A sly, unpleasant smile made her mouth a little less perfect in shape as the new arrival said, "Please do excuse my riding habit, Lady Pennsfield. I was in such a hurry to see dear Darcy that I rode Tristram over from Foxmere rather than wait for my carriage."

She moved into the room as if she owned it. Alicia took an instant dislike to the woman. She had an air of flaunting defiance that grated on her.

"Silly old Etta said you weren't receiving guests to-day, Lady Pennsfield. I do wonder sometimes how you put up with her. She's getting too old to follow orders."

From outside the room came a gasp of outrage. Etta could be seen peeking in, her face mottled with rage.

Still no one had said a word. The woman struck a pose and cried, "Ah, tea! I should dearly love a cup."

Lady Pennsfield's reply was withering. "As Etta made it, I dare say it wouldn't be to your taste."

No move was made to introduce the newcomer. Alicia glanced at Miss Austen, who seemed as puzzled as she was.

Finally the woman in scarlet said, "Do introduce me to your friends, ma'am."

Alicia could see that the dowager was having difficulty keeping a rein on a temper that no doubt could be as formidable as her son's.

Forced by the rules of etiquette to perform the introductions, her ladyship said in an almost strangled tone, "Miss Austen, Miss Fitzhugh, Lady Beatrice Underhill."

The new woman took one look at Jane Austen and dismissed her out of hand; but her eyes narrowed when she looked at Alicia, as if she recognized her as the enemy. Then she turned to Lord Pennsfield, who sat as if turned to stone. He had not even risen when she entered.

"Well, Darcy, no greeting for me?" The voice was coy, cloying, but with an underlying bite of acid.

For a moment Alicia thought he wasn't going to answer. His face was drained of color, and he seemed struck dumb. Then he rallied.

"I trust you don't expect my mother, Lady Pennsfield, to receive your gamekeeper husband!"

"Husband? What husband? Surely you don't think I married Lambert, do you? I eloped with him for an adventure—I'd scarcely marry so far beneath me."

Lady Beatrice, having exploded her bombshell, flounced out, leaving a stunned audience behind her.

CHAPTER SIX

THE RIDE BACK to the manor from the Dower House was silent. Alicia thought surely his lordship would make some explanation of the explosive scene with Lady Beatrice Underhill; but he devoted himself to driving the phaeton faster than was wise with a broken arm, so that Alicia had to cling to the side of the high seat to keep from being tossed to the ground. She longed to take the ribbons herself, but knew this would only further incense his lordship, so she kept a tight rein on both temper and tongue, although it taxed her sorely to do so. He pulled the team up so abruptly that one of the horses reared. Fortunately a groom ran out, caught the horse's head, and calmed it.

"Well, what are you waiting for?" Pennsfield roared at the young lad. "Boy! Help Miss Fitzhugh down." A footman was coming down the steps to assist her, but Alicia decided not to wait for him. She accepted the groom's rather grubby hand and alighted from the phaeton speedily. She'd scarcely set foot onto the drive before Pennsfield whipped up the team and went careering off, gravel spurting from the wheels.

"Cor, miss, 'is lordship's in a rage, ain't 'e?" the groom said, wide-eyed at the performance. "'e'll break t'other wing if 'e ain't careful.'' He walked off toward the stable block, shaking his head.

Alicia found Fanny waiting to assist her in changing clothes. One look at the plump little maid and Alicia knew the entire servants' hall must be rife with rumors. As Fanny put away the leghorn hat, she was already chattering.

"Oh, miss, you can't imagine what happened while you and his lordship were taking tea with Lady Pennsfield." Her eyes snapped with the gossip she could scarcely contain. "We had a caller here at the manor."

"Was it someone interesting?" Alicia inquired. "Not someone calling on me, of course. No one knows me in Derbyshire."

"Oh, no, miss. A lady called on Lord Pennsfield." She rolled her eyes dramatically. Perhaps she'd missed her calling and should have been a comic actress on the stage.

"Then she can scarcely concern me," Alicia replied, but not rebukingly, for she was very curious to hear what the staff thought of her ladyship.

"It might affect you, miss." Fanny gave her a judicious examination and nodded. "You're much too pretty to suit her. Much. You may lose your position, worse luck."

This did ring alarm bells. Although she and Pennsfield didn't always deal well together, Alicia was settling in here. She'd not met any likely suitors yet; but Lady Pennsfield's offer to obtain invitation cards to Chatsworth was promising.

"Why should I lose my position as secretary? His lordship's arm won't be out of the splint for weeks." When that time came she'd have to do something about finding another place; but she'd think of that later.

"It's Lady Beatrice, miss. It was she who came calling today, bold as brass, to see the master. Rode over from her own place, without so much as a groom to accompany her."

"Lady Beatrice?" Alicia pretended ignorance. "Isn't that the lady who—"

"The same, miss. Left him waiting at the church." Fanny giggled. "Usually it's the other way around, isn't it?"

"But I thought you said she eloped."

"With her gamekeeper. But I was talking with Alfie in the stables after she'd gone. He'd been to the blacksmith's in Bakewell this morning and met an undergroom from Foxmere. Told him the whole story. After she'd given him all kinds of expensive gifts, the gamekeeper left her for a barmaid he met up in the Lake country. She came home in a royal rage, she did. Shouted at all the servants. Now I guess she's going to try to get his lordship back again."

Remembering how Lady Beatrice had raised her hackles, Alicia exclaimed, "Surely he'd not take her back after such a public humiliation."

"I don't know, miss. They're making wagers in the hall. Some think he'll give her the go by. Others bet he'll be dangling after her in no time. Plenty feel she'll be mistress of Pennsfield Manor before the year is out—" she lowered her voice "—worse luck."

"You don't relish the thought of Lady Beatrice as your mistress?"

"Those in service at Foxmere wish they could go elsewhere; but any who dare leave must go without a letter from her. Oh, miss, she can be nasty when crossed."

Remembering those bold, arrogant eyes, Alicia believed Fanny's assessment of Lady Beatrice's character. Although she found Pennsfield overbearing and every bit as arrogant as his former betrothed, she felt almost sorry for him. If Lady Beatrice got her hooks into him again, she'd reel him in like a Highland salmon.

"Well, I'll be long gone from Pennsfield Manor before anything can happen," she said to Fanny. "I'm here only until his lordship can hold his own pen again."

"That could be quite some time, miss. Me mum broke her arm once and she couldn't use that hand for ever so long. Had to exercise it, working up to holding things gradually. You might well be here for Christmas."

Alicia knew Fanny was right about one thing. She'd not be here long if Lady Beatrice came back into Pennsfield's life. That look she'd gotten from her had been a telling one.

NEXT DAY his lordship was cross as a baited bear.

"I'm sure that's not the word I dictated," he grumbled. "Have you been altering my prose again, Miss Fitzhugh?"

"Indeed, sir, I have not. Believe me, I should never use such an infelicitous phrase as that."

He slapped the page down on his mahogany desk. "Were you so critical of your other employers?" he asked, his voice dangerously low.

"I worked for ladies previously, sir."

"And?"

Alicia shrugged prettily and noticed that his angry eyes strayed to her bosom, which was artfully revealed by a piece of Belgian lace she had tucked into the rather low-cut neckline. Ordinarily she wore more modest gowns when she was working with Pennsfield; but today she'd decided to put on this pretty morning dress of green sprigged muslin. Her motives were not to be examined too closely.

"You find you cannot work well for a man?"

"Have you not found my work satisfactory, sir?" It amused Alicia to see him scowl when she answered a question with another. It was rather refreshing to find a man who wasn't catering to her every whim.

"I find you excessively impertinent at times," Pennsfield growled, exasperated. "It's not easy to dictate my stories when I am used to penning them myself."

"Indeed, my lord, I'd not thought of that. What a hoddy-doddy I am, not to realize it would be difficult." She thought of her own correspondence. Alicia had always preferred to write her own letters, even though many of her friends employed indigent women relatives to take over this task. "There's little you can do, though, except use a secretary until your arm heals."

He leaned back and ran his left hand through his long, thick blond hair. As usual, one lock escaped his fingers and fell back over his forehead. That pale blond lock was beginning to give her incessant trouble. When he barked orders at her, she wanted to pull it until he yelled. But when he talked to her as a friend or tugged at it in a frenzy of balked creation, she wanted to smooth it with her own hand.

"Indeed, Miss Fitzhugh, I have been in a foul mood today, which must put you at a disadvantage."

"Any disadvantage is negligible, sir,"

"But I should not let my personal feelings interfere with business. I shall try to deal better with you in the future."

"And I, sir, shall try not to be so—was it impertinent?"

A little smile lightened his gloomy countenance. "That was the word."

"And you prefer meek, mild women who never disagree with you."

"Life's more placid with them."

Alicia couldn't help smiling at this. "Sir, I cannot imagine you in any placid situation, in either of your personae." She picked up one of his published novels. "Lady D certainly doesn't write placid situations into her books."

"But that's fiction," he protested. "Who wants to buy a book with no conflict in it? Conflict is what makes the story interesting."

"My lord, I rest my case. You are arguing it for me."

He glared, then burst out laughing. "Impertinent again."

During the next day or two his mood kept changing so rapidly that Alicia was sometimes almost afraid to speak to him, for fear he'd cut her off with a curt, sarcastic reply. When he did this, it got her back up, and she was always tempted to answer him in kind, but the better understanding between them, intermittent though it was, pleased her too much to be sacrificed to the momentary pleasure of a setdown.

One morning a few days later, Pennsfield stopped dictating in midsentence and asked, "Do you ride, Miss Fitzhugh?"

"Of course."

"My brain is full of cobwebs. If you have a riding habit with you, I suggest we go out for a ride. It is much too nice a day to be cooped up inside."

Alicia wanted to shout with joy, for she had so missed riding. In London she rode nearly every day, meeting her friends as they cantered along Rotten Row in Hyde Park. Then she remembered his broken arm.

"Can you ride with your arm still immobile?"

This inquiry immediately broke the rapport between them. In high dudgeon, he snapped, "Don't keep treating me as if I were a child still in leading strings, Miss Fitzhugh. I am quite capable of deciding if I am able to ride."

"Of course, sir."

"Well, are you going to change or not?" he demanded. "I shall see you at the stable block. But if you take hours to primp and preen before your mirror, then I shall ride off without you."

"I shall hurry," she promised, almost running from the room. Alicia was torn between annoyance at his impossible ways and the chance to go riding. Riding won, and she rang for Fanny to help her into her habit.

"His lordship is going riding! Oh, miss, what about his arm?"

Alicia paused long enough to say, "When I brought this up, Fanny, he gave me orders not to treat him like a child."

"Have you noticed that he's much more fidgety since Lady Beatrice came back to Foxmere? Do you think he still loves her?"

"What nonsense! After the way she treated him?" Alicia was highly indignant. "I've met this notorious Lady Beatrice. She is not quite the thing, Fanny."

"But men sometimes don't see through such women, miss."

"His lordship isn't a fool, Fanny. He was quite cutting to her when they met."

"They're still making wagers in the hall."

"Oh, bother the servants' hall, Fanny. Don't be such a chatterbox. His lordship is waiting to go riding."

Properly chastened, Fanny held her tongue as she helped Alicia into a bright green habit finished down the front with black braiding. The sleeves were slightly puffed at the shoulder, then they narrowed to braid-trimmed cuffs.

"Do you want the little cork round hat, miss?"

"Yes, and my leather boots and Limerick gloves."

Catching up the skirt, Alicia hurried down the stairs and out the side door of the manor to the stable block, where she interrupted a heated exchange between his lordship and a grizzled old fellow in a groom's leathers.

"I told you to saddle Satan," Pennsfield thundered. "Do you expect me to ride this rocking horse? It might do for Miss Fitzhugh, but not for me."

"Yer can't manage Satan with one arm, milord," the groom said with the familiarity of a lifelong servant. "This bay's safe enough."

"Give it to Miss Fitzhugh."

"Bill's saddling up Flower for the lady, milord."

"Odbert, saddle Satan," Pennsfield thundered.

The elderly groom just said, "Here, sir, I'll give you a leg up on Rebel. You'll get a good enough ride for your first time in weeks."

Pennsfield glared and made no move to mount the horse. A stable lad brought out a sweet little gray mare for Alicia, so Odbert came to give her a leg up. When his back was turned to his lordship, the groom looked up at Alicia and muttered, "See if you can keep him from breaking t'other arm, miss." Then he tossed her into the saddle with the ease of long practice.

"Odbert, I can dismiss you," Pennsfield threatened, blond brows drawn into a straight line, lips thin with rage.

"Indeed you can, milord. Now—" he cupped his hands into a step "—up you go on Rebel. Remember, I've been handling horses since before you were out of skirts. You can get your own back at Satan once you've two arms to control him."

Alicia was amused at the confrontation. This time she knew Odbert would win. Old family retainers usually got their way in such situations. As Flower pranced, eager to be away, Pennsfield growled, "I should give you the sack," and put one booted foot into Odbert's hands. It probably galled him to use any assistance to mount; but with one arm out of use, he had little choice.

They cantered down the long driveway under a canopy of lime trees that met in dappled green arches over the road. The air was pleasantly cool with a little breeze sighing through the hedgerows of haw. Soon Pennsfield turned off the road onto a narrow path that led into a copse of ancient beech, drawing up Rebel when they emerged in a grassy clearing full of bracken. A brook gurgled along, and finches sang in the thicket bordering the water.

"What a lovely place," Alicia exclaimed. "I am more accustomed to riding in Hyde Park than in the country."

"A pity," Pennsfield said, a devilish gleam in his blue eyes. "I'd thought we might ride cross-country."

Alicia had hunted frequently when staying at country houses; but this was not the time to tell him she could cross a fence with the best of them. She remembered Odbert's warning, so she played the timid miss.

"I'm better on bridle paths than over hedges." Her mouth watered for a good race, but common sense told her she must curb such longings. If he was thrown again, the results could be dangerous. "Perhaps, later, when I've had more experience in riding over broken country..." She forced herself to add, "I'm not the best rider in the land."

He gave her such a shrewd look that Alicia wondered if he suspected she was gammoning him. "You ride quite well, Miss Fitzhugh." Then, moving closer to her, he added, "It is such a bore having to call you Miss Fitzhugh. So formal when we're together so much. Do you think it would be proper for us to use Christian names when no one else is near?"

Alicia pretended to give this proposal serious thought, although inwardly she was laughing. Being an underling was such a nuisance at times—particularly when she was suddenly cast as an inferior after years of giving orders.

"You may address me as Morgan if you like."

"Thank you . . . Morgan." His mouth twisted as if he'd bitten into a green persimmon. "I do wish your given name was more . . . more feminine."

"I am sorry, my lord, that I cannot accommodate you in that matter."

"Now, now, no more of this 'my lord' when we're alone. My name is Darcy."

Alicia had had to school her mind to think of him as Lord Pennsfield in case her tongue should slip. What a relief it would be to allow herself to think of him as Darcy! Solemnly she responded, "Very well, my—I mean, Darcy."

Again he gave her a sharp look, making her wonder if he suspected something. She had already sent off a letter to Hon Zella, warning her that Lady Pennsfield would be writing to her. What bad luck to wind up in the one place in Derbyshire where someone knew her godmother.

Darcy shook Rebel's reins and led the way out of the clearing. Soon the country opened to a beautiful vista of hills, green fields marked with hedgerows and manor houses tucked into wooded parks.

"How I'd relish a good gallop," Darcy said.

As if he had evoked the sound, they heard the thud of galloping hooves coming from ahead of them, beyond the tall hedges. Then a familiar figure rode into view, veil streaming in the wind behind her, skirts ablow, a flash of scarlet brightening the greens of the landscape.

Darcy reined in Rebel so abruptly that Alicia feared he would unseat himself. Her lovely day dissolved as Lady Beatrice saw them and pulled up her own mount in a display of spirited horsemanship.

"Darcy, what a coincidence. How nice to see you riding again." She came close enough to eye his mount, then made a moue. "Riding that old hack? How dull." She ignored Alicia as if she did not exist.

With surprising courtesy, Darcy said, "Miss Fitzhugh is not such an experienced rider as you, Beatrice. I was afraid she'd not be able to keep up if I rode Satan."

It took all of her willpower to keep Alicia from gasping in outrage. Silly chit. She could outride her any day.

"How boring for you, Darcy," Lady Beatrice purred, turning a smug smile on Alicia. "Miss . . . is it Fitzpatrick?"

"Fitzhugh," Alicia said, icicles hanging from each syllable.

Lady Beatrice shrugged off the name as unimportant. "The road back to Pennsfield Manor is just around the bend. I'm sure you can manage to get back to the stables alone." Then, imperiously, never doubting she'd be obeyed, she cried, "Come on, Darcy, let's see if that old nag can take a fence."

Alicia might not have existed. Darcy accepted the challenge, dropping the reins on the horse's neck and using his crop to send Rebel into a gallop.

"Fool!" Alicia cried. "You'll break your neck." She could have admitted defeat and ridden back alone to the manor as Lady Beatrice had ordered; but Alicia was made of sterner stuff. The day she took orders from Lady Beatrice Underhill, she'd be ready to give up the ghost. Flower took no urging to race along after the others. Alicia watched in terror as Lady Beatrice sailed over the first stone wall, a flash of scarlet exploding in exuberance. Crouched low over the neck of Rebel, Darcy cleared the wall easily. Moments later, Alicia sailed over it, delighted with the horseflesh under her. Flower was a born jumper.

After five minutes of this, though, Darcy reined in. Just as Alicia caught up with him, Lady Beatrice sensed that she rode alone and came galloping back.

Winded, his face pale as if his broken arm ached, Darcy panted, "Enough for the first time out, Beatrice." Then, noticing Alicia, he said, surprised, "How did you keep up?"

"An interesting question, Darcy," Lady Beatrice commented, eyes narrowed as she looked with suspicion at Alicia. "Didn't you say this person was your secretary? Then what is she doing riding cross-country with you? Why isn't she in your study, doing whatever it is that secretaries do?''

Alicia waited for Darcy to defend her, but he sat silent. Unable to hold her tongue, she retaliated. ''I'm riding with his lordship to make sure he doesn't make a fool of himself and break more than his arm.''

The minute she said it, Alicia regretted her rash words, for Darcy was glaring at her as if she were his enemy.

''I'm quite able to take care of myself, Miss Fitzhugh. I daresay you've had enough riding for one day. Perhaps it would be better if you returned to finish the work on your desk. You can find your way back alone?''

''My sense of direction is quite good.'' She tugged at Flower's head and cantered off, back stiff with anger. How dare he treat her like a servant? She hoped he did take a fall. It would serve him right—and that insufferable vixen in scarlet, too.

CHAPTER SEVEN

"MISS FITZHUGH, Lady Pennsfield would like you to join her in the Green Room for tea."

"Thank you, Vernon. I shall change quickly."

"If you please, miss," the butler said, "her ladyship has been waiting for some time. I'm sure she will excuse your riding habit."

It was a command audience, so Alicia went straightaway to see Darcy's mother. She hoped her ladyship wouldn't ask too many personal questions. She was loath to lie, but she did not want to give away her position, either. What a coil!

The Green Room was a charming sitting room with green velvet wall coverings and a deep green carpet. The furniture was French, delicate and graceful, all white and gilt. Her ladyship looked up when Alicia entered and curtsied to her.

"Please forgive my costume," Alicia murmured. "I have just come in from riding and did not wish to keep you waiting."

"You look charming, Miss Fitzhugh. Please join me for tea." She rang and waited until the downstairs maid had served them and left the room before she came to the point of her visit. "Vernon told me that you and Pennsfield were out riding. I was alarmed. Is he able to ride yet?''

Remembering his mad gallop with Lady Beatrice, Alicia replied, ''He seemed to manage rather well, ma'am, although I was afraid he might have been too bold for the first time astride since his accident.''

''My son is very strong-willed, Miss Fitzhugh, as you may have discovered.''

Alicia chose not to answer that; but her silence was eloquent.

''I do hope he'll occupy himself for a time. I instructed Vernon not to tell him I was here.''

''You may rest unworried, ma'am. He did not return to the manor with me.''

Alarm showed in the patrician features. ''And pray where is he? He is well, is he not? You're not keeping anything from me so that I will not worry?''

''Oh, he was well when I was dismissed, ma'am. He had met more felicitous company and no longer needed me to try to keep him from breaking more of his bones.''

''And just who might this other company be?''

''Lady Beatrice Underhill.''

''Oh, fie! Why did that trollop have to come back here?''

Again Alicia chose not to reply, although she concurred wholeheartedly with Lady Pennsfield's sentiments, including her assessment of Lady Beatrice's character. ''Trollop'' was the perfect description of Lady Beatrice Underhill.

''Miss Fitzhugh, I need your help,'' Lady Pennsfield said. ''Although you are working here as my son's secretary, I recognize quality when I see it. I shall not ask you how it happens that you must earn a living. I know all too well that women of quality sometimes fall on hard times. Sometimes their fathers gamble away their living. You impress me well, Miss Fitzhugh.''

"Thank you, ma'am." Alicia felt faintly alarmed. What was all this leading to?

"The fact that Gisella Montague recommends you is proof enough for me that you are out of the top drawer." She sipped her tea, as if giving herself time to collect her thoughts, to marshal her arguments. "I am very worried about my son, Miss Fitzhugh. When he told me that he intended to wed Lady Beatrice Underhill, I was appalled. I knew he'd been squiring her to balls and seeing quite a bit of her, but I thought he had better sense than to consider matrimony. The woman is fast. She has had a reputation of being loose since she came out. At the time I thought he would come to his senses, so I said little, afraid that any opposition might make him stubborn. He can be stubborn, you know,'' she added ruefully.

"Indeed I know," was Alicia's wry reply.

"Too late I realized Darcy intended to go through with this...misalliance. By then there was nothing I could do to stop the wedding. My dear Miss Fitzhugh, you can't know how happy I was when that trollop jilted him." She nibbled a dainty sandwich. "Tea is so refreshing at midmorning, I always say, more so than coffee or chocolate. But I digress. I am determined that hussy shan't have my son. Obviously she has changed her mind and expects to take up with him again.''

Alicia nodded agreement.

"Her gamekeeper!'' Lady Pennsfield's lip curled in disgust. "And now she expects Darcy to make her his wife.''

"Quite possibly.''

"We shall thwart her, Miss Fitzhugh.''

Little alarm bells rang in Alicia's mind. What did this formidable woman plan? She wanted no part of any scheme involving Darcy, although she had to admit, it would do her heart good to score off the hateful Lady Beatrice.

Cautiously she probed for Lady Pennsfield's meaning. "What did you have in mind, ma'am? A bit of ground glass in her saffron cake?''

"My dear, you joke. But there have been times in the past few days when such drastic measures have crossed my mind. I think you and I in tandem can do better than that without putting ourselves in jeopardy. Lady Beatrice Underhill isn't worth the noose.''

"Indeed not, Lady Pennsfield.''

"I wish to noise it around—oh, very discreetly, so that it will reach Lady Beatrice's ears by such a circuitous route that she'll never find the source—that Darcy is pledged to another.''

Alicia saw the pit yawn at her feet. "Surely you don't intend to link his name with mine!''

"Why not, Miss Fitzhugh? You are eminently suitable.''

"Your son and I don't deal well together. We're constantly at odds. No one who is with us for five minutes will believe such nonsense."

"Not nonsense at all," the dowager snapped. "Those who know Pennsfield best know he doesn't care for simpering little women without a thought in their silly little heads."

"On the contrary, ma'am, that is exactly the kind of woman he extols."

"Oh, tosh! He's only gammoning you, Miss Fitzhugh. He's not escaped marriage this long by dangling after such women. They are as plentiful as bluebells in the Highlands. No, he wants a woman of character. He may not realize this himself—"

"Obviously not, if he chose to marry Lady Beatrice."

"Don't underestimate her. She has fire and character. It isn't the kind of character I wish to see brought into the Cummings family, but there's naught vapid about her. She is shrewd and cunning. I will not have her for a daughter-in-law."

"I'm sorry, ma'am, but I cannot lend myself to such a scheme. I dread to think what would happen if his lordship heard such a rumor."

"He never pays any attention to gossip. If he had, he'd have known what that vixen, Beatrice, was before he proposed."

"Has it ever occurred to you that he knew but did not care?" Alicia asked, bringing up her big guns to shoot down the dowager's scheme.

"Miss Fitzhugh, you insult my son's considerable intelligence."

"Unfortunately, men often leave their intelligence in a bandbox when it comes to choosing a life's companion. They heed their emotions, not their minds."

"She cast a spell over him," Lady Pennsfield insisted.

"If so, she's weaving another. I fear she'll soon have him in thrall again. He left me for her today without a backward glance." Alicia wasn't aware of the bitterness that crept into her tone.

The dowager gave her a telling glance. "Methinks you are miffed by today's episode, Miss Fitzhugh."

"She'll have him over every fence in the county, ma'am. He was getting tired. I could see it. But all she had to do was beckon, and he followed like a puppy."

"That's why we must work at countering her spell, my dear. You are the best material with which I can work. If you will just put your mind to it, you can snatch him from under her nose."

This had gone on much too long. "Lady Pennsfield, I do not want your son."

"Not want him! But he's the catch of Derbyshire. All the mothers invite him to their balls, hoping he'll cast his eye on their daughters."

"Then choose one of them for your scheme, ma'am."

"He has a considerable fortune," the dowager said suddenly in a wheedling voice.

"Good God, do you think me a fortune hunter?"

"No, no, of course not; but a rich husband isn't to be sneezed at, Miss Fitzhugh."

"Can't you just hear Lady Beatrice telling every one that I'm after your son for his money?"

"Who cares what she says?" Lady Pennsfield said airily.

"I care."

The elderly lady scowled exactly as her son did. "I had hoped you'd see things my way, Miss Fitzhugh. You can't want him making a fool of himself over that trollop again."

"That is not my concern." Alicia was quite firm. "I am here temporarily, only as his secretary, until his arm heals."

"Fie, woman, surely you can't wish on my son such a fate as marriage to that Underhill woman!"

"I repeat, it is not my business to interfere in his lordship's life."

"The Cummings men have always married quality," she insisted, holding up her proud old head.

"Cheer up, ma'am, he's not married yet. Perhaps she'll jilt him again."

"I fear not. She has learned her lesson. Now she thinks to make a respectable marriage. She will become Lady Pennsfield over my dead body."

Alicia wouldn't be moved. She didn't like Lady Beatrice, but she'd take no part in this wild scheme to keep Darcy out of her clutches. Remembering how he had dismissed her in such a cavalier manner, Alicia spitefully hoped he would marry Lady Beatrice. He deserved her.

"Well, I regret that you think so little of my idea," Lady Pennsfield said, acknowledging defeat. "I had thought perhaps Miss Austen—but when I met her, I knew my son would never dangle after her. Not that she isn't of impeccable character, and she has a fine mind; but she's too quiet for him. He needs someone with more fire, someone who won't put up with his temper, who'll set him down when he needs it." She sighed. "Someone like you, Miss Fitzhugh."

"I should think you'd want someone out of the top drawer for him." Alicia knew she must keep reminding Lady Pennsfield that she was a lowly secretary. If the old woman ever suspected the truth, she'd ferret it out and broadcast it all over Derbyshire. "I am of the middle class."

Lady Pennsfield made no comment, but her look spoke volumes.

"I shan't keep you from your work longer, Miss Fitzhugh. I don't for the life of me see how Darcy can have so much correspondence!" This probe Alicia ignored. "Oh, you will be receiving a card from the Duchess of Devonshire soon. Her ball is in two weeks. Pardon me for prying, but do you have a suitable gown with you? If not, it would give me the greatest pleasure to send you my own dressmaker—as a gift to you." She gave Alicia a stern look. "Now, none of your stiff-necked pride. I don't know what Darcy pays you, but it can't possibly stretch to a proper ball gown."

The offer of such a munificent gift did call up Alicia's considerable pride but she decided that accepting it would be more in keeping with her character of penniless secretary, and might help in keeping the dowager away from her insane plan to pass Alicia off as Darcy's betrothed. In any case, she'd left her best gowns at home.

"It is exceedingly kind of you, Lady Pennsfield. You are right in thinking my wardrobe does not run to ball gowns. If I am too prideful to accept your kind gift, I shall shame you at Chatsworth."

"Good. I shall send Mrs. Bigby to you tomorrow. She subscribes to *Ackermann's Repository* and has the latest fashion plates from Paris." She eyed Alicia critically. "Something striking but restrained, and in a color. Lady Beatrice always dresses to be seen. We'll outshine her—but tastefully. You, my dear Miss Fitzhugh, have elegance."

On that note she finally allowed Alicia to leave her.

Alicia quickly changed into a plain round dress and hurried down to the study to do some copying. As she came to the bottom of the stairs, she heard her nemesis.

"When the cat's away, the mice will play. Really, Darcy, you should be firmer with the servants. In fact, I really don't see why you need Miss Fitzsimmons—"

"Fitzhugh," Alicia corrected icily.

Lady Beatrice shrugged. "Miss Secretary will do. But I could write your little notes for you, Darcy."

Alicia saw the look of panic that raced over Lord Pennsfield's face before he schooled it to blankness. *Aha, he had not confided his literary secret to Lady Beatrice.* The novels of Lady D had been sold in bookshops for several years. So he'd not seen fit to take his betrothed into his confidence even before the notorious jilting. How very interesting.

Deciding he needed a setdown for being rude to her while riding, Alicia smiled sweetly at Lady Beatrice and murmured, "Indeed, Lord Pennsfield, I do seem redundant now that Lady Beatrice is back. Shall I tender my resignation? I'm sure she is clever enough to do all your work.''

She thought she might have gone too far this time, for he seemed to swell with rage, but with a visible effort he managed to contain his temper. ''I think you'd find the work excessively boring, Beatrice, and your pretty hand would cramp from writing. Haven't you told me you have your Cousin Prue to do all your notes for you?''

''But I'd be helping *you*, Darcy,'' Lady Beatrice cooed. The look she gave Alicia would have wounded had it been a dagger.

''No, no, don't even think of such a thing. I don't want your violet eyes tired. They might lose their lovely sparkle.''

And what about my eyes? Alicia thought, disgruntled. The silly fool of a man, besotted by Lady Beatrice's all-too-earthy charms. Had the man no pride? Was he going to take a gamekeeper's leavings? What fools men could be! And his fond mama wanted to marry him off to her—or pretend to. What an insult! Who would want Darcy Cummings, Baron Pennsfield? Let Beatrice Underhill have him, and good riddance.

''If you'll please let me pass, Lady Beatrice, I must get back to work. As you pointed out, that's what I'm paid to do.''

She flounced past them and marched to the study, back as straight as a ramrod. She made a great show of closing the door.

She heard all too clearly, though, Lady Beatrice's hateful voice pitched to carry. "Really, Darcy, where did you find such an insolent, insubordinate woman? She'll have to go."

CHAPTER EIGHT

"I HAVE HAD MY ORDERS from my mother that you should have time off from your work to have a ball gown constructed by her jewel of a dressmaker, the redoubtable Mrs. Bigby."

Alicia protested, "Surely the seamstress's hours can be arranged so as not to interfere with your book."

"Miss Fitzhugh, when my mother issues an order, even I dare not say no to her."

Miss Fitzhugh. What had happened to his own suggestion that, while at work, they should be Morgan and Darcy? Now she must return to calling him Lord Pennsfield. She was immensely piqued by being forced to take this step backward in their relationship. All this new formality stemmed from the reentry of Lady Beatrice into his life, and Alicia resented the influence that lady had on him. It wasn't that she herself wanted him. Indeed not! He was much too opinionated, too pigheaded, too stupid—that was the word—for her taste. Still, it galled that he should dangle after Lady Beatrice. No matter what his faults, and they were legion, he deserved better than that trollop—to use his own mother's favorite contemptuous term.

"I promise you, sir, I shall not slight your work."

"As you can see, my work isn't going well," Darcy fretted. "I wish I could hold a pen again. This dictating isn't to my liking."

"I thought you had been doing quite well dictating."

"Well, I haven't." Darcy glared as if it were her fault that his arm was broken, and ran his hand through his hair, leaving it faintly disheveled. One pale blond lock fell down over his brow, and Alicia wanted to smooth it back into place. Pity—that was all she felt, she told herself sternly. He really was in a pretty coil, with his work suffering because of a woman not worthy of him.

"Is there anything I can do to help your work along?" she asked, eager to get his book flowing again.

"Just stop badgering me!"

"My lord, it is shabby of you to vent your ill humor on me," she said coldly and distinctly. "If my work is not satisfactory, tell me so. I have already offered to resign."

"Oh, bother. Why did God invent women? Think how pleasant the Garden of Eden must have been before He tampered with poor Adam's ribs."

"I'm sorry I cannot oblige you by turning into a man" was Alicia's starchy comeback. "Although what one's gender has to do with taking dictation and making fair copies, I do not know. I've known many a man who couldn't write a legible hand, or spell 'cat' without making a mistake."

"You always have to take me up on the slightest remark," Darcy complained, quite as though he was the victim of an unprovoked attack. "Why must you have such a prickly nature, Miss Fitzhugh?"

"Really, sir, I do not have a monopoly on prickliness."

In the silence that followed, Alicia brooded over thoughts of going back to London and letting this insufferable man stew in his own juice. He couldn't ask Lady Beatrice to write for him, lest his secret be found out by everyone in the county. It would serve him right if Lady Beatrice Underhill led him a merry chase and, finally, after she had caught him, put him on a lead fastened to a ring in his nose. Then he'd find out what women really could be like!

Darcy got up from his desk and paced the floor. Alicia was reminded of a caged bear she'd seen once. The only word that described both was "surly."

"I'm going out. Transcribe what I've given you, and then Mrs. Bigby can occupy you with plans for an entire wardrobe." He stalked out of the room as if all his misfortunes were her fault, hers alone.

"Good riddance," she muttered, turning to her work, which was finished in short order, as he'd dictated scarcely two pages that morning. If he kept this up, he'd not satisfy his publisher, and Alicia knew he'd blame her. If he dared do that, she'd pack her boxes and leave that very day.

From the window of her room, she saw Darcy ride out on Rebel, presumably on his way to Foxmere. Downcast by his unfairness, Alicia sat down and penned a letter to Hon Zella, the first complaint she'd written since her arrival at Pennsfield Manor. She characterized Darcy Cummings in this epistle as overbearing, stupid and caustic. She wrote of Lady Beatrice Underhill, sure that Hon Zella knew the latest *on-dits* about her. After she'd vented her spleen for several pages in her elegant copperplate hand, Alicia tore up the letter and began again. Hon Zella would only say "I told you so" to her complaints. Instead, she mentioned the ball at Chatsworth and confided to Hon Zella her fear that she would encounter someone who knew her there. Chatsworth would be crowded with the ton. But short of feigning illness, she couldn't wriggle out of the ball—and besides, she was longing to go.

Mrs. Bigby arrived that afternoon with a drab little girl to assist her and a lumpish lad to carry in bolts of exquisite fabric. The seamstress was built like a partridge, plump and gray, her own dress not at all stylish. It took Alicia only minutes to discover, though, that the woman knew her business. She had Alicia stand and turn around, then walk about the room to "see how you move, miss." Then she snapped her fingers at Kate, demanding the fashion plates.

"With your carriage and dark beauty, something striking," Mrs. Bigby said. "Not pastel. Everyone at Chatsworth will wear pastels." Another snap of impatient fingers, and the young man laid bolts of fabric about the room for her inspection. Then she dismissed him, giving him orders to stay within call, not go running out to natter with the stable lads.

"I have just the style for you, Miss Fitzhugh," Mrs. Bigby declared after her sharp-eyed inspection. Another snap of the fingers, and Kate fanned out the plates as if she were performing card tricks. The dressmaker selected one, looked at it carefully, looked again at Alicia and then nodded. "This will do admirably for you, miss." She bustled about the room, cocking her head to one side at each bolt of fabric and puffing from her exertions. Finally she lifted the free end of a length of India muslin and said, "Please come here, Miss Fitzhugh, so I can hold this under your chin to consider the color."

Alicia obeyed, delighted with the choice, for it was a bright poppy-red and she knew she could carry off the rich color with her dark hair and gray eyes. Mrs. Bigby unrolled enough of the fabric for her to drape it under Alicia's chin, motioning for Kate to hold it in place while she stepped back to get the effect. She nodded, satisfied.

"Perfect, miss. Not many could carry off a dress of that color without looking like a Gypsy. On you, when I finish it with gold lace, it will be soigné."

Alicia took the fashion plate and examined it closely, delighted with the sleek, understated style. The corsage was fitted, with an elegant stomacher of double rows of gold lace extending up to the shoulders, which were cut quite low. Bands of gold lace trimmed small puffed sleeves, and the cuffs of the lace matched a band around the high waist. The skirt flared more than usual and had a broad wadded hem to make it stand free. The bottom of the skirt was trimmed with more gold lace. It was plain but very elegant, and Alicia fell in love with it.

"Will it do, miss?" the dressmaker asked; but her tone made it clear she knew the style would be exactly right for Alicia. "You are tall and slender enough to carry it off, but you have a lovely bosom. The style wouldn't look right on anyone flat-breasted."

"It's perfect," Alicia breathed, taking the length of fabric from Kate so she could turn and see the effect for herself in a free-standing full-length mirror.

"Then if you'll take off your gown and petticoats, we'll do the measurements, miss."

Alicia made a resolve. She would take that insufferable Darcy Cummings away from Lady Beatrice. She didn't want him; he was much too prickly for her taste. But she'd been insulted by that...that trollop, and she was determined that Lady Beatrice shouldn't have him.

She stood patiently while Mrs. Bigby used her tape measure and muttered measurements to Kate, who jotted them down in a notebook. During this time Alicia decided to write immediately to Sally and have her send a whole trunk of gowns. She was declaring war on Lady Beatrice, and she needed her full complement of armor to do battle.

The next week was hectic, for Mrs. Bigby returned for several fittings of the ball gown, and they discussed suitable accessories. Alicia chose a turban made of the poppy muslin with gold lace trimming, and she had her own shawl of the finest blond lace which Mrs. Bigby pronounced just the thing to set off the ensemble. The dressmaker fingered the delicate silk lace and murmured that it was of exceptional quality. If she wondered how a mere secretary could afford something so obviously expensive, she held her tongue. No doubt she thought it had been the gift from some gentleman for favors rendered. It amused Alicia to realize she had probably been cast in the role of scarlet woman.

She wondered what Lady Beatrice would wear to the ball, for she assumed her ladyship would be there. Although Lady Beatrice was not of good character, she did own Foxmere and was still received by most of the toplofty families in Derbyshire. Knowing the woman's flamboyant taste, Alicia was prepared for anything. She did know Darcy wasn't to escort Lady Beatrice to the ball. By chance, while strolling in the garden one afternoon, she'd overheard an argument between Lady Pennsfield and her son. They weren't quite shouting at each other, but as they were in the drawing room and the doors were open to the garden, their voices carried as if they were on the stage at the Drury Lane Theatre.

"I expect you to escort us to Chatsworth," the dowager was saying in that tone of command that brooked no denying.

"Sorry, mama, but I have other plans."

"Cancel them. You certainly do not expect me to make my own way there! And I have two guests who must be escorted."

Alicia had to smile. The day Lady Pennsfield needed to be taken anywhere was far in the future. That redoubtable lady was quite capable of traveling to the Continent alone. Alicia recognized her strategy. The dowager was separating her son from his sorceress.

Alicia moved away, not wanting to be caught eavesdropping; but she felt sure Lady Pennsfield would win the evening. She couldn't keep Darcy away from his Beatrice once he arrived at Chatsworth; but at least he would not come in with Lady Trollop on his arm. Alicia allowed herself a daydream. He might escort her. She knew he looked elegant in formal attire, for he was tall and carried himself like a prince—and he was unquestionably handsome. Even his black silk sling didn't detract from his good looks. If anything, it added to his allure.

Then she stopped short—whatever was she thinking of? She and Darcy were at daggers' points most of the time. They had just about reached rapprochement when Lady Beatrice made her entrance and all the good feeling between them had vanished. Well, if she meant to thwart Lady Beatrice, Alicia knew she must reestablish that pleasanter feeling betimes.

But how? His work was suffering. There were days when he paced the study, not dictating a single word. If she said anything to him, he snapped and snarled like an angry hound, and his anger seemed always to focus on her. No matter what she said, he took exception to it.

When she approached the study the next morning, she went prepared. Her trunk had arrived the day before, and she'd had Fanny working overtime ironing her dresses. She could see the question in the maid's eyes as she hung the lovely gowns in the wardrobe. Fanny was knowledgeable enough about fine dresses to know that they were scarcely attire for a secretary. Alicia sighed. No doubt the servants would be all abuzz, wondering how she'd acquired such finery. The more spiteful ones would certainly think she'd been a kept woman. Perhaps Darcy would think so, too.

Would that change his attitude toward her? She smoothed down the skirt of her pink muslin round dress, knowing the color was very becoming. The dress was quite modest, for the collar was high, with a double pelerine attached to it. Long, full sleeves hid her arms. It was the color that set this dress apart from her usual working clothes. Today she had dressed her hair high and wore a pretty Parisian cap that tied under the chin with pink ribbons. The upstairs maid had brought in a bowl of primroses, and Alicia took a small bouquet of them and pinned them to the top of the cap.

When she walked into the study, Darcy was reading his manuscript, a frown on his face. He held a pen awkwardly in his left hand and had just jotted something down as she entered. He glanced up at her. His blue eyes opened wide momentarily, and there was a look in them she recognized, having entertained a long list of suitors through the years since her come-out. It was admiration.

"Good morning, sir."

Instantly he was back to being her employer. "You are going out this morning? I thought perhaps we could do some work on this manuscript for a change."

Alicia remembered her resolve. She'd never catch him with vinegar. It was time for honey. Giving him a quizzing look, she replied quite innocently, "No, sir, I have no plans other than work." Demurely she crossed the room to her own small desk and sat down, eyeing him alertly. "Are you ready to dictate, my lord?"

He gave her a withering look. "I thought we had agreed to informality here in the study, Morgan. Now

I find you calling me 'my lord' as if I'd never told you my name.''

How dare he? It was he who had gone back to calling her Miss Fitzhugh. She wanted to pick up the pretty crystal inkstand and throw it at him; instead, she pasted a smile on her face and murmured, ''I'm sorry, Darcy. I forgot.''

''A good secretary doesn't forget things,'' he said severely.

''I'll try to do better,'' she simpered.

''So why are you dressed up this morning?''

''I? Dressed up, Darcy?'' She dropped her long, dark lashes. ''This old dress?'' She opened her eyes, a picture of injured innocence.

''I've not seen it before. You never wear pink.''

''But it's summer, and I felt like wearing something cheerful. Don't you like it? If not, I will change it. To gray, perhaps?''

''And waste more time? Never mind. I have the new chapter blocked out in my head and I want to get it down before I lose it completely.''

He was back in harness and dictated rapidly for more than an hour. Then he stood up, stretched and looked over her shoulder.

''What's that you're writing?'' he demanded. ''It looks like gibberish.''

In order to keep up with his dictation, Alicia had been taking shortcuts. ''It is just abbreviated words, Darcy.''

''No wonder I keep finding changes in my text. You can't read what you scribble down, so you make up something. It won't do. It won't do at all, Morgan.''

Her back stiffened at his newest calumny. In her starchiest tone, she announced, "I can read it perfectly, even if you can't." To demonstrate, she read back to him what he had just dictated.

"I didn't say it that way," he muttered.

"You most certainly did. I have a very retentive memory."

"Well, it doesn't sound right," he grumbled.

She turned and looked up at him, with a saccharine smile. "You're right, it doesn't. I've been trying to tell you exactly that about your novels for some time now."

He snatched up the last page she had written, crushed it in his hand, and threw it back onto her desk. "I am tired of your impertinence!"

"And I'm tired of your unfair accusations!"

He stamped across the room and stood glaring out of the French windows, opened now to catch the morning breeze.

"You would try a saint's patience, Morgan."

"Then isn't it fortunate that you're no saint?"

He turned quickly and tried to stare her down; but steely eyes met flashing blue ones steadily. Then, to her surprise, he flung back his head and roared with laughter.

"Impertinent, impudent—but you do keep the blood racing, Morgan. Life with you is not dull."

"I should hope not, Darcy," she said demurely, smiling inwardly, hopeful that this was the end to his moping and pining for Lady Beatrice.

"Shall we declare a truce?" He strode across the room and held out his hand to her.

She put her own hand in his. Her fingers tingled at his touch. All her willpower was needed to keep her hand there and not snatch it away.

"Let's go riding," he said, retaining her hand a moment longer than was necessary for a friendly handshake, eager as a boy to escape the schoolroom. "It's much too nice a day to be cooped up with fool-scap and inkwell."

Alicia remembered the disastrous ride they'd taken previously. Darcy had declared a truce earlier—and the battle had been rejoined before the day was out. If she was to take him away from Lady Beatrice, though, she'd have to forget his past actions and build on present goodwill. "I'll change into my habit immediately, Darcy."

They had a delightful ride, with no unwelcome interruptions. Darcy rode sensibly; he did not show off for her. He even commented on her riding habit, one of the costumes that had arrived from London. It was slate-gray and done in the military style, trimmed with black braid and with braid epaulets at the shoulders. A charming little cocked hat of black beaver completed the effect, with a gauzy veil of mint-green to give a bit of color.

Her pleasure in the ride and Darcy's company, for he'd been charming and witty the entire time, was diminished when she was changing out of her habit on their return.

Fanny, with her unerring nose for gossip, said, "We'll be seeing more of his lordship the next few days."

"Oh?" Alicia's black brows rose, questioning.

"Lady Beatrice coached off to London yesterday for a visit. Playing hard to get, I shouldn't wonder."

So that's why he asked her to go riding. Bother! It took most of the joy out of her day. Why couldn't Fanny keep her gossip to herself?

On the other hand, it gave Alicia some time to consolidate her improved position with Darcy. She'd make the most of it.

CHAPTER NINE

THE WEEK BEFORE the ball at Chatsworth flew by pleasantly. Lady Pennsfield hadn't mentioned again her wild scheme to introduce Alicia as Darcy's intended wife. Alicia and Darcy were on cordial terms, and his book progressed at a great rate. Lady Beatrice was still in London, so he took Alicia riding on most days.

The day before the ball, though, he didn't suggest a ride. Later little Fanny, the gossip monger, reported that Lady Beatrice was back from London, where she'd had a gown made for the ball. Alicia's spirits fell. During their work session that morning, Darcy had been preoccupied. No doubt he knew of Lady Beatrice's return. Alicia had hoped she'd stay in London. She should have known that Lady Beatrice wouldn't miss such a special social event as a ball at Chatsworth.

Lady Pennsfield had announced that Miss Austen would join them. "The present Duchess of Devonshire is highly intellectual," the dowager confided to Alicia. "She will appreciate both Miss Austen's writing and her keen wit." Alicia was looking forward to seeing Miss Austen again. At least if Darcy spent his entire evening with her rival, she would have someone to talk to.

When she donned her new ball gown, though, Alicia's spirits soared. It was one of the most elegant dresses she'd ever owned, and she knew it was exceedingly becoming.

"Oh, miss, you look like a duchess!" Fanny exclaimed, her sparkling brown eyes wide with delight. "You will be the belle of the ball. That Lady Beatrice won't hold a candle to you."

"Thank you, Fanny." Alicia adjusted the poppy-and-gold turban a fraction of an inch to show a bit more of her raven hair, then fluffed the short *coquelicot* feather attached to it. Fanny handed her French trimmed gloves that matched her white satin shoes. A charming little fan of peacock feathers completed the ensemble.

A tap at the door, and a footman announced that the landau was waiting. Swirling her exquisite lace scarf about her shoulders, Alicia went down the main staircase to where Darcy waited for her.

She didn't hurry but stepped regally, delighted at the look on his face when he saw her.

"Morgan! You look stunning. I'll be the envy of every man at Chatsworth."

He looked rather stunning himself, she thought, in his evening clothes. The points of his snowy collar were high, brushing his cheeks, his neckcloth exquisitely folded. He looked completely at ease in his square-cut coat with a white satin waistcoat buttoned high. He had chosen the new fitted pantaloons, which were strapped over black dancing pumps, and wore an evening cape of black satin lined with white, which gave him a dashing look. As Alicia had expected, even the black silk sling for his broken arm enhanced his glamour.

Briefly she could bask in his admiration. When they reached Chatsworth and Lady Beatrice—well, she'd see.

Lady Pennsfield was elegant in a gown of black crepe figured with black satin, while her guest, Miss Jane Austen, wore a very pale green, which was most becoming.

The ride through the long twilight to Chatsworth was delightful. Darcy chatted with all three ladies, putting himself out to be charming. He asked Miss Austen how her writing was coming, and she told him her final revision was well in hand. "You are sure you don't mind my using 'Darcy' for my hero's surname, sir?"

"Indeed, it may make me famous, Miss Austen," he quizzed, smiling pleasantly.

As the coach began the final approach down the hill through the park surrounding Chatsworth, Alicia had her first look at that magnificent mansion. The warm stone glowed in the distance; the river beyond made the vista immensely attractive.

Seeing her interest in the scene, Miss Austen murmured, "Now you see why I have chosen to pattern Pemberley after this."

"Indeed I do, Miss Austen. It is enchanting."

They now joined a long line of carriages, all bound for the mansion that lay like a jewel in a setting of green. It was weeks since Alicia had been to a glittering social function, and she was looking forward to this ball. She had missed her social life and had longed to escape Pennsfield for balls and parties at which she might meet the man who would love her for herself. She found that she was stealing glances at Darcy—so handsome, so suave. He seemed to have two personalities. This evening there was no sign of the caustic temper, the belittling manner, that she'd grown accustomed to when they worked together.

The first crack in her pleasure came in the ladies' cloakroom, where the three of them retired to make sure their coiffures had not been disarranged during the carriage ride. As they went into the charming chamber, Alicia heard a voice say, "I understand Pennsfield is escorting his secretary."

Another spiteful voice added, "Secretary? Isn't that a polite word for mistress?"

A calmer tone chimed in. "Ladies, ladies, the rumor is that they are secretly betrothed."

Indignant, Alicia turned on Lady Pennsfield; but that lady assumed an innocent mien. "I told you I wouldn't be a part of your charade, ma'am. This is unkind of you."

"My dear, I don't know what you mean. No doubt someone has seen you and my son out riding, and assumed . . . you know how it is."

Exasperated, Alicia muttered, "Yes, I know exactly how it is." She only hoped the story wouldn't reach Darcy's ears. She could only shudder to think of his reaction to such an *on-dit* as that.

Lady Pennsfield moved off to greet friends, and Miss Austen murmured, "Has her ladyship set afoot some scheme to thwart the flamboyant Lady Beatrice?''

"You have guessed it, Miss Austen.''

"Please call me Jane.''

"And I'm—Morgan.'' She almost identified herself as Alicia. How criminal impersonators ever kept their different identities straight was a puzzle.

Word seemed to spread through the rooms that Alicia was present, for there were many covert looks in her direction but no more audible remarks about Darcy's secretary.

"I hate to have my reputation smudged in this fashion,'' Alicia complained to Jane.

"My dear, ignore them. Small minds thrive on gossip. Although I must admit, it sounds as if you are living in an exciting novel.''

Alicia's new friend continued, "One can scarcely blame Lady Pennsfield for trying to extricate her son from the coils of Lady Beatrice. My one brief meeting with her was quite enough for me to judge that she's not the thing, not the thing at all.'' She smiled a wicked little smile at Alicia. "While you, dear Morgan, are obviously out of the top drawer.''

Stubbornly, Alicia insisted, "I am but a secretary, Jane.''

"I sense a mystery here, Morgan. No, don't deny it. And men are attracted to women of mystery. I do believe you would be a much more suitable choice for his lordship than Lady Beatrice.''

"Oh, fie! Such nonsense. You're quizzing me, Jane.''

"Wouldn't you like to give her a setdown?" Miss Austen asked, a scheming look in her dark eyes. "She really was quite discourteous that day at Lady Pennsfield's."

"And worse when I went riding with Dar—Lord Pennsfield."

Jane gave her a sharp look.

Now Lady Pennsfield caught them up and swept them out to be presented to the Duke and Duchess of Devonshire.

Darcy joined them and they moved toward the Painted Hall, where the dancing was to take place. His lordship delivered their cards to the majordomo, resplendent in livery and powdered wig. This august figure rapped the floor with his staff and intoned loudly, "The Lord Pennsfield, The Lady Pennsfield, Miss Jane Austen, Miss Morgan Fitzhugh."

When she made her curtsy, Alicia saw a familiar gleam in the duke's eye. He might be in his sixties, but he had always liked the ladies. The duchess was gracious and told Miss Austen she hoped to have a chat with her later about her writing.

To her combined delight and dismay, Darcy offered his arm to Alicia rather than to his mother and led her into the spectacular Painted Hall, the ceiling and upper story of which were decorated with scenes from the life of Julius Caesar. The lower story was ivory-painted wainscoting, the floor a magnificent black-and-white checkered marble.

There was a buzz of interest as Darcy led Alicia onto the dance floor. The musicians, who were tucked away on a balcony at the end of the great hall, struck up a waltz. Even with only one hand, which he placed at her waist, Darcy was a marvelous dancer, and they dipped and swirled about the floor until Alicia was almost giddy with pleasure.

At the end of the waltz, she discovered that her escort was surreptitiously scanning the crowd.

In a sudden fit of pique, she murmured, "She's not here yet. Believe me, Darcy, if she was, everyone in the room would know." Immediately she could have bitten her tongue, for Darcy glared down at her, all the rapport they'd built up through the week gone.

As if on cue, the majordomo announced, "Lady Beatrice Underhill."

Without a word, Darcy led Alicia back to where his mother sat with Miss Austen, bowed formally and moved toward the entrance to the Painted Hall. Chagrined, Alicia sat down, her eyes glued on his back.

"Oh, bother!" exclaimed Lady Pennsfield. "I hoped she would not attend the ball."

Alicia didn't bother to respond. Nothing on earth would have kept Lady Beatrice at home tonight.

Then a gasp went over the assembly of guests as that lady entered the room. Alicia's eyes popped open with shock. She knew her rival was flamboyant and that she was reputed to be fast. She knew of the escapade with the gamekeeper. She'd seen her in her scarlet riding habit. None of this prepared Alicia for what she now saw. To all intents, her ladyship was nude. She wore a flowing Grecian style, which had been popular a decade earlier during the height of the classical revival, but had quickly gone out of fashion. It was made of sheer aerophane crepe, an airy, crimped, almost transparent fabric. Under it was a petticoat of the finest lawn, which she had dampened so that it clung to her generous curves as if glued on or applied with a brush.

In a whisper calculated to carry throughout the immense room, Lady Pennsfield said, "Strumpet!"

If Lady Beatrice heard, she paid no heed, for Darcy had just reached her and made his bow.

"He'd better not dare bring her over here," his mother said, tight-lipped with fury. "I shall cut her dead."

Alicia was sick at heart. She'd had a chance and had muffed it. Why couldn't she learn to control her sharp tongue when she was with Darcy? She knew too well they were like flint and steel; sparks always seemed to fly when they came in contact with each other. For her, the evening, which had loomed so pleasantly, was now ruined.

Miss Austen leaned close and whispered behind her fan, "Don't be so downcast, Morgan. It won't last. He's too intelligent to form any lasting alliance with such as she."

"On the contrary, he's completely stupid where Lady Beatrice is concerned. Remember, he was waiting at the altar for her when she jilted him for her gamekeeper. Obviously he has not learned a thing."

"I will not have it," the dowager raged. "She shall never be mistress of Pennsfield Manor."

Short of murder, Alicia couldn't think of any way to prevent it.

Then, to complete her disastrous evening, she looked up and saw coming toward her, eyes agleam, none other than Quincy Rawson, late of London. With a sinking feeling, Alicia knew she was about to be unmasked.

Murmuring, "Please excuse me, ma'am," she rose quickly and moved toward Quincy, hoping to prevent his calling her Lady Alicia within her ladyship's hearing.

His blue eyes lighted up when he saw her standing before him. "I say, Lady Alicia—"

"Shh!" she cautioned. "We must talk privately."

He gave her a very quizzing look, but bowed and then offered his arm. "I daresay we can find a quiet corner, my dear." They moved away from the dancers and stepped into an adjoining salon, finding a corner where no one could overhear them.

"Well, Lady Alicia, what are you up to?" he asked bluntly. "I heard the majordomo announce you, but the name he used was not yours. What game are you playing up here in the wilds of Derbyshire?"

What to say to this blockhead? She'd have to take him into her confidence without actually telling him anything.

Leaning toward him slightly and holding her pretty peacock fan so that no one else could see her face, Alicia murmured, "Quincy, you must help me. If I am unmasked, I shall be ruined. May I count on you as a dear friend?"

Hers was the right approach, for she could see him swell with importance. "I am at your service, Lady Alicia."

Trying to be as mysterious as possible, Alicia whispered, "I cannot tell you all the details, Quincy, for the honor of others is at stake. Suffice it to say that I am here incognito.''

"What was the name they gave you? It had a faintly familiar ring.''

"Morgan Fitzhugh. Miss Morgan Fitzhugh. As to its sounding familiar, I am Lady Alicia Morgan Fitzhugh St. John. So it truly is my name—at least, a part of it.''

"How beastly clever of you, Ali—Morgan." He corrected himself with a conspiratorial smile.

"So, will you pledge not to reveal my secret?" she coaxed.

He placed a hand over his heart dramatically. "My lips are sealed, Alicia—Morgan. Damned if it isn't hard to remember your new name.''

"I'm sure you'll manage nobly, Quincy," she purred.

"I hear a waltz. Shall we dance?"

"Delighted, sir." Now, if this stupid oaf didn't give away the game . . . What horridly bad luck for him to be here. "How does it happen you're here at Chatsworth?''

"Cousin is getting married next week, and I'm here for the festivities." They moved back into the ballroom. As Quincy swung her about the room, he asked, "I say, Morgan, who is that Lady Beatrice someone who is wearing the spectacular gown?''

"Lady Beatrice Underhill," Alicia said coldly. "And what you call spectacular I call making a spectacle of herself. She might as well parade au naturel.''

"She certainly has many charms on display. Who's the fellow with her? The one with the broken wing? Handsome devil. Lucky fellow, that."

And I hope it's all bad luck, Alicia thought with spite. "That's Darcy Cummings, Lord Pennsfield."

"Oh, I say! My cousin passed along an *on-dit* about him. I gather he's the talk of Derbyshire these days. Is that delectable creature with him his secretary? Can't be. Not her ladyship."

Alicia froze momentarily, missing her step. "Sorry," she murmured.

"Talk is that he has a *tendresse* for his secretary," Quincy went on, as usual completely unconscious of his partner's feelings. "The secretary certainly must be a nonpareil if she beats that bit of femininity."

"As you are so interested in Lady Beatrice, perhaps you would like to meet her," Alicia suggested smoothly at Quincy.

"You are acquainted with her? I should be delighted to meet her, Al—Morgan."

"Do try to remember my name, then," Alicia scolded with acerbity. "Otherwise my honor and that of others will be smirched."

"On my own honor, Morgan. Morgan doesn't quite suit you, though."

"Well, that's how I'm known here. I'm on a mission of some delicacy."

"The Prince Regent?" he muttered.

"I must not reveal anything," she whispered back, delighted by this interpretation of her cryptic remarks. "Well, come along, the waltz has ended. You shall meet Lady Beatrice. She has a large fortune, Quincy.''

Quincy's eyes lit up.

Darcy scowled as Alicia moved up to join him and his clinging companion. For a second she hesitated, sure that this hostility stemmed from the rumors about them that were flying around the room, but seeing him bristle at Quincy's stare of open admiration for Lady Beatrice, she murmured, amused by the knowledge that much of this blatant interest was for her lady-ship's fortune rather than for her all too obvious feminine charms, "May I present the Honorable Quincy Rawson? Lady Beatrice Underhill. Lord Pennsfield.''

As the orchestra struck up a gavotte, Quincy bowed and asked, "May I have the honor of this dance, Lady Beatrice?''

Lady Beatrice saw Darcy's scowl and smiled sweetly at Quincy. "I should be honored to dance with you, Mr. Rawson," she murmured.

A demure manner didn't fit her, Alicia thought unkindly.

Without a word to Darcy, Lady Beatrice took Quincy's arm, and they moved off to the dance floor. Darcy looked like a thundercloud ready to spew lightning.

"Who is he?" Darcy demanded.

"Quincy? He's a son of the Earl of Stafford.''

"And how do you know him?''

"I made his acquaintance in London." She owed Darcy no explanation of Quincy Rawson.

"Does he have any chance of inheriting the earldom?" Darcy probed further.

"Quincy? Hardly. He's the fourth son."

"Aha! A pauper. Does he know that Beatrice is rich in her own right?"

"As he is visiting in the county, no doubt he knows."

"She should be warned he's after her money."

"Really, Darcy, you worry too much." Alicia turned to leave him and go back to his mother, but he took her firmly by the waist and swept her out onto the dance floor. "Is he a good dancer?" Darcy asked, craning to see the interesting couple.

"He is an excellent dancer, and quite handsome, too, don't you think?"

"Weak face. What can she see in him?"

"There's no accounting for tastes," Alicia replied dryly.

Later, in the ladies' retiring room, a furious Lady Beatrice confronted her. "You sly puss," she hissed, keeping her voice low so that only Alicia could hear her. "Betrothed to Darcy? Obviously he isn't as smitten with you as you might suppose. He came looking for me the moment I arrived."

Alicia, rigid with anger, let her cool gray eyes travel over Lady Beatrice. "He could scarcely miss seeing you. Did he appreciate your baring yourself to every male eye at Chatsworth?"

"I'll not let you have him. He'll be mine for as long as I want him."

"And then you'll discard him again, I suppose. Poor, stupid Darcy, he'll never learn," Alicia said lightly. She'd not give Lady Beatrice the satisfaction of knowing she was angry. "Take him away from me if you can," she challenged

CHAPTER TEN

"So you have already told Mr. Rawson that Lady Beatrice has a fortune," Miss Austen stated, eyes sparkling.

She and Alicia were taking tea in her pleasant room at the Rutland Arms in Bakewell. Darcy had business there today, so he had asked Alicia if she wished to drive in with him. Naturally, she had agreed. The week had been very odd, with Darcy blowing hot and cold. Some days it was as if Lady Beatrice didn't exist. Other days he was cross and moody. He had never mentioned the rumour about his betrothal, and it seemed that everyone at the ball had heard it but he.

Something about Jane Austen inspired confidence, so Alicia talked more freely with her than with anyone else in Derbyshire. She had not gone so far as to tell her new friend that she really was Lady Alicia St. John, but she had been frank about her thwarted scheme to detach Darcy from Lady Beatrice.

Now the writer put her fertile mind to work, seeking a solution for Alicia's troubles. "You know that this man from London is a fortune hunter."

"Oh, yes, I know" was Alicia's dry reply.

"I've heard there's another such right here in the county. Sir Hilary Ingham of Ravenswood."

Alicia nodded. "I met him the first evening I was at the manor." She smiled, remembering. "Apparently Sir Hilary was a frequent visitor to the manor; he even used to come to dinner uninvited. That evening he twitted Darcy about Lady Beatrice. At that time I'd not met her. Darcy flew into a rage and gave him such a setdown that he's not been back."

"Too bad we can't send him in pursuit of Lady Beatrice, too," Jane mused, eyes narrowed in thought. "Just to keep the pot boiling, you understand."

"Now that Darcy is back with Lady Beatrice, other men may think twice before dangling after her. He can be most formidable when angry." She smoothed down the skirt of her French gray bombazine carriage dress. "Besides, Sir Hilary lives here. He knows Lady Beatrice all too well."

"It is surprising he's not tried to marry her. After all, her fortune is considerable."

"With Darcy in the running, why would she even look at Sir Hilary?"

"You actually care for Lord Pennsfield, don't you?"

"Me? Care for Darcy? He's pigheaded, opinionated, stubborn, irascible, ill-tempered—"

"Ah, Morgan, methinks the lady doth protest too much."

Alicia felt her cheeks grow hot. "We don't deal well together."

"Sometimes you do," Jane reminded her. "And you certainly are more suitable to be Lady Pennsfield than that person from Foxmere."

"Darcy doesn't think so. He tolerates me only because I write a fine hand and he needs a secretary." Not even Miss Austen could be told that Darcy was Lady D. Fleetingly Alicia wondered how he would keep his secret after he wed Lady Beatrice.

"Surely you aren't going to sit back and let that unlovely creature have Lord Pennsfield? Morgan, where is your fighting spirit?"

"He would never choose me. Remember his cruel remarks when we discussed the plot of your novel? He thinks it wrong to marry outside one's class."

The look Jane gave her was very shrewd. Did she suspect something? Alicia could only hope that Quincy hadn't given her away. He could easily blurt out her secret without meaning to, and then the fat would really be in the fire.

"Morgan, forgive me for being blunt. I don't know what your circumstances are. I understand you must earn your living. But I have met many types of people. As a writer, I have honed my skill at reading character. You may now be impecunious, but you have known better times. You would grace Pennsfield Manor and never bring shame to it. Don't let that impossible woman have him." Miss Austen smiled her sweet smile to soften her words. "I must agree with Lady Pennsfield. You are a better match for her son than Lady Beatrice Underhill."

"She doesn't really want me for a daughter-in-law," Alicia protested. "I'm just to be a kind of stalking horse to keep Darcy away from Lady Beatrice."

"I wouldn't be too sure of that. She talked to me of you in glowing terms, Morgan, the night of the Duchess of Devonshire's ball. Apparently she knows some friend of yours."

"Yes. One of my…patronesses." How Alicia hated to lie to this new friend. But if once she began telling the truth, it would eventually get back to Darcy. His finding she had tricked him would put paid to any chance of friendship between them. He'd turn to Lady Beatrice in spite, if nothing else. Inwardly Alicia shuddered. She'd been foolhardy to embark on this adventure. Now she was caught in the coils of her own plot and didn't know how to extricate herself.

"I still think there must be some way to get Sir Hilary Ingham into the game," Jane insisted. "The more men chasing the flamboyant Lady Beatrice, the more chance for her to tire of your Darcy."

"Not my Darcy, Jane." He would never be hers. The time would come when she'd have to tell him who she truly was, and that would be the end.

On the way back to Pennsfield Manor, Darcy surprised Alicia by asking, "Would you like to take the ribbons, Morgan? You've bragged that you were a good whip. Now we'll see."

Luckily she had some fine Limerick leather gloves tucked into her reticule. She drew them on and reached for the reins, delighted to try her hand at the spirited cattle drawing the phaeton. She'd never driven a high phaeton before, but that didn't disturb her. She'd had her first pony cart at the age of six and had been driving ever since.

When they came to a straight stretch of road that had a good surface, she gave a little smile of glee, flicked the whip and was elated at the response of the matched pair. She took one quick look at Darcy, seeing surprise in his blue eyes. Then she concentrated on her driving, racing along at a great rate until they neared the old humpbacked stone bridge crossing the brook, where she slowed to a reasonable pace. As they swept up the long drive to the manor, Alicia's cheeks still flushed from exhilaration, she saw admiration on Darcy's face. Stopping with a flourish, she relinquished the ribbons to him as one of the stable boys hurried out to hold the heads of the horses.

"I must admit you are the finest lady whip I've ever seen," Darcy said. "Where did you learn to drive?"

She smiled coquettishly. "Here and there."

"Always the woman of mystery, eh, Morgan?" He swung down from the phaeton and came around to assist her. "Sometimes I wonder about you."

"Do you, Darcy?"

"Someday I'll learn your secret," he warned.

His words chilled her heart. That was the day she dreaded.

As they went into the hall, Darcy suggested tea in the small drawing room, a charming place with walls paneled in a light wood and furniture upholstered in soft blues and greens to rest the eye. After the maid had brought their tea, Darcy began, "I've become too much of a recluse. I think I'll have a small dinner party, if you will be good enough to address the invitations."

"Part of the duties of any good secretary, Darcy."

"I never know when you're quizzing me and when you're serious, Morgan," he complained playfully.

"Feminine secrets are not for men to know," Alicia riposted, pouring more tea for him from the Minton teapot. "Have you a guest list ready?"

"Do you think your friend Miss Austen would attend? I would send a carriage for her."

"I daresay she'd be pleased to come."

"And what about that fellow I met at Chatsworth—Rawden? Rawly?"

"Quincy Rawson?" She was surprised that Darcy would invite someone so obviously interested in his lady love. "Mr. Rawson is a bit like your friend Sir Hilary Ingham. A free meal is a free meal."

"I thought he was a good friend of yours, Morgan. Shall I not invite him?"

She looked at Darcy in surprise, caught off guard by his implication. "Do you mean that I am to attend this dinner party?"

"Of course. I scarcely think you'll be hard pressed to use the proper etiquette, Morgan," he said dryly. "Someday," he warned, "I'll find out why you are working as a secretary."

"One must eat," she said piously, but the look he gave her told Alicia that he wasn't taken in.

"Well, shall we have this friend of yours who is not a good friend?"

"Why not? He is a pleasant dinner guest." She didn't add that it fitted right into her plans to try to interest him further in Lady Beatrice and her in him.

"As to Ingham, I'm afraid I rode roughshod over him the last time he was here—your first night at the manor."

"I remember. You were rather beastly to him, Darcy." But she smiled to soften her rebuke.

"That should be a good number—three ladies, three gentlemen."

"Three ladies? Miss Austen and I make two. Who else?" As if she needed to ask.

"Lady Beatrice, of course." He looked at her as if she were the village idiot. "Sometimes, Morgan, I wonder if your brains have been scrambled." He was back to his old caustic manner. Why hadn't she kept silent? She knew very well, without asking, that Lady Beatrice would be invited.

"If you think I'm an idiot, then you must spell out your instructions clearly," she said coldly. "I am not a mind reader, Darcy. I have no crystal ball or fortunetelling cards, no means of divination."

"Why is it that every time we seem to begin to deal together with some degree of civility, you must say something to spoil our rapport?"

"I say something?" she hit back, indignantly. "I think it is you who always spoils our friendship."

"I hate women who always try to put the blame for everything on the man."

"That's unfair, Darcy. Do you know how many times in every day I must bite my tongue from answering your slighting remarks?"

"Perhaps you should keep a tally" was his cutting answer. "I begin to wonder if this dinner party is a wise move."

So did she, but for once Alicia held her tongue. He continued to make plans for the dinner, so it seemed that his misgivings had not caused him to change his mind.

Later that day, when she was looking for the early part of his latest romance, she couldn't find it. "Darcy, I don't see the first chapters of—"

"Oh, I sent that off by the mail to the publisher to keep him happy. He's been pressing for the manuscript."

He should have told her. As his secretary, she should have been the one to send it for him. "Who addressed the parcel?" she asked.

"I had Nestor do it." No explanation as to why he'd not ask her to do it. Didn't he trust her?

Later that day they received a summons from Lady Pennsfield to take tea with her, one of her usual command audiences. Darcy wasn't happy at the prospect. "I suppose she'll lecture me on my association with Lady Beatrice," he muttered.

Alicia kept very quiet.

"Well, won't she?" he challenged, belligerent.

"I cannot know what her ladyship will discuss with you, Darcy," she said, trying for calmness. It wouldn't do for him to hear a reproving note in her voice.

"You'd think I was still a child in skirts," he grumbled.

Alicia firmly resisted the obvious riposte. He gave her a telling look that made her wonder if he could read her mind.

"You haven't much to say today, Morgan."

"As anything I say seems to displease you, I am trying to keep silent," she snapped, annoyed beyond endurance. He was deliberately provoking her, and she knew it and he knew it.

"I shall be glad when my arm is out of the sling," he said balefully.

"And so shall I. I would have left long since had I not felt honor bound to fulfill my obligation to do your writing for you."

"Indeed, if any other applicant had answered my advertisement . . ." He didn't bother to finish the sentence.

Alicia sighed. They were back at the beginning again. Why had she thought they might deal well together? She'd even thought briefly that Darcy might be the man for her, the man she'd longed to find. What a ninnyhammer she'd been to entertain such an outrageous thought. He was impossible.

They drove down to his mother's house in a gig with only one horse between the shafts, a sweet goer. There wasn't a hack in his stables. Darcy certainly knew and appreciated good horseflesh.

When she commented on the animal's good qualities, he said, "I go to Horncastle to the horse fair most years. The Gypsies bring in the finest cattle in England."

The dowager was in high good humor, which surprised Alicia, for she had expected fireworks over Lady Beatrice.

"I've just been reading the London *Gazette*," her ladyship said as she poured tea for them. "Our friend, Gisella Montague is mentioned in connection with a curious piece of gossip."

Alicia was startled and had to catch herself before she made some revealing statement. Hon Zella as an *on-dit*? It was incredible.

As Hon Zella was supposed to be her patroness, Alicia knew she must say something, or Lady Pennsfield would think it passing strange. "And what has the Honorable Gisella Montague done that sets London ton on its ear?"

"It's more what she's not done" was the cryptic answer. Alicia sensed that the dowager was playing this for all it was worth for some purpose of her own. It made her uneasy. Now what was this wicked old woman up to?

"Come, Mama, don't keep us hanging," Darcy said indulgently. He, too, recognized his mother's dramatic technique. "What has this old friend of yours been up to? Something scandalous?"

"Indeed not" was the indignant reply. "I've just had a charming letter from her, renewing our acquaintance."

Alicia cringed mentally. She knew she could trust Hon Zella not to give away her masquerade; but clearly Lady Pennsfield sensed a mystery concerning Alicia, and she had the tenacity of a bulldog.

Peering through her lorgnette shortsightedly, Lady Pennsfield read, "The Honorable Gisella Montague is keeping very silent about the whereabouts of her goddaughter, Lady Alicia St. John, who has mysteriously disappeared from the London scene. Impoverished male members of the ton particularly miss the heiress."

"Probably got tired of fortune hunters and left for the Continent," Darcy said. "Can't say I blame her. Must be a nuisance, having men dangle after you for your money."

Alicia thought it wise to make no comment. The dowager had given her such a shrewd look that she wondered if that redoubtable woman suspected the truth. However, if she did, she made no move to reveal her knowledge but steered the teatime conversation to other topics. Not once did she mention Lady Beatrice. Perhaps she was wise enough to know that any disapproval would only make him more stubborn.

CHAPTER ELEVEN

THE DINNER PARTY did not provide a particularly felicitous evening. Alicia was on pins, fearing Quincy would call her Alicia instead of Morgan. Sir Hilary, who was supposed to pay attention to Lady Beatrice, still kept giving Alicia thoughtful looks. Miss Austen tried hard to keep a literate conversation going, but it wasn't easy. Lady Beatrice was brittle, and her gaiety seemed forced, while Darcy brooded, not doing much to keep the party alive. Alicia felt the tension crackle and wondered if they would survive the dinner party without an explosion.

At least Darcy had chosen to entertain in a small salon, where the servants had set a round table, so that there was no question of who sat at the head of the table, who sat at the foot as hostess.

"Write me place cards, will you, Morgan?" Darcy had requested that afternoon.

"What seating plan do you want?"

"I'll attend to it," he had said.

She'd given a little shrug, done the cards, and given them to him without comment. Later she found he'd put Lady Beatrice on his right, Miss Austen on his left. Beside Beatrice, he put Quincy, with Sir Hilary beside

Jane. This put Alicia between the two other men and directly across from him.

Alicia had dressed with care for this party. She chose to look elegant, wearing an understated dress of pale blue twilled sarcenet, the front simply ornamented with four satin bands that formed a stomacher. The sleeves, short and full, were arranged in festoons by four satin buttons. The skirt had a border of satin roses, which were echoed with smaller roses on each shoulder. Tonight she wore her sapphire pendant and earrings. Reckless, perhaps, for no mere secretary would own such jewels; but they set the gown off to perfection.

Miss Austen arrived first, as Darcy had sent a carriage to Bakewell for her. She, too, was elegant in white *Gros de Naples*, the gown a simple round dress ornamented with satin and pearls.

Quincy and Sir Hilary arrived within minutes of each other. Darcy learned they had made each other's acquaintance in previous encounters. Alicia was a bit amused, for the two fortune hunters eyed each other suspiciously. Perhaps it took one to spot one. Now, if only they'd pay court to Lady Beatrice, it would please Jane, who was convinced that would help to keep things at a fever pitch.

"Where is Lady Beatrice?" she whispered to Alicia from behind a pretty little ivory fan.

"Maybe her carriage overturned," Alicia said hopefully.

Unfortunately, the lady arrived just then. Alicia had hoped she'd be at her flamboyant best, which gave a chance for advantageous contrast; but it seemed that

Lady Beatrice had learned a lesson at the Duchess of Devonshire's ball. Tonight she wore a black crepe dress over a black sarcenet slip, the modest bodice of white crepe very tastefully trimmed with vandykes of black velvet. A white crepe toque adorned with white roses and a chastely designed diamond necklace completed the effect.

Alicia had trouble doing justice to the feast. Cook hadn't stinted on the courses, and they moved from fish to fowl to a joint of beef, a country-cured ham and a saddle of mutton. The men and Lady Beatrice ate heartily.

She'll be fat if she keeps on eating at that rate, Alicia thought uncharitably. Already Lady Beatrice was showing the first faint signs of a double chin, and a few more pounds would make her more than pleasingly plump.

The men didn't seem to mind. Both Quincy and Hilary devoted themselves to her, to the extent that even Darcy realized his duties as host and engaged Jane in conversation about her book.

"Oh, an authoress!" squealed Lady Beatrice. "Dear me, we must watch what we say and do, or Miss Austen may put us in her book! Do deal kindly with me in print, dear Miss Austen," she trilled, to Alicia's disgust.

"I always disguise my characters, Lady Beatrice," Jane assured her. "Otherwise, I would have no friends."

Alicia had a premonition that all was not well with Lady Beatrice. It wasn't until the sweet, a pudding cunningly shaped like a porcupine with slivers of almonds for quills, that lightning struck.

As she spooned up the delicacy, washing it down with copious mouthfuls of wine, she gave Alicia a look of pure loathing. Then, turning to Jane, she said, "I have the most delicious plot for your next novel, Miss Austen."

Alicia saw the expression that flickered over Jane's face, to be suppressed immediately. She guessed that this was one of the bad aspects of writing novels—everyone wanted to give you a story. However, Jane said politely, "Indeed?"

"We have a wealthy man, quite a catch, in fact. Not too young"—did she look pointedly at Darcy?—"but still good-looking. He has had a disappointment in love and is on the rebound."

Alicia saw Darcy's face close as if he'd pulled shutters over it. She could see what Lady Beatrice was up to. Sir Hilary knew. Lady Beatrice didn't care. No doubt Quincy would soon catch on. From the tiny moue of distaste Miss Austen made, Alicia knew she was all too aware what devilment Lady Beatrice was perpetrating.

"He hires a woman—not too young, rather on the shelf—to do his correspondence for him, as he has injured his hand." She gave a sly look at Darcy and seemed pleased at his stolid face. "Soon, although they are completely unsuited to each other, word circulates in the neighborhood that they are betrothed." She paused for dramatic emphasis, then went on, "The poor man has no idea that she's telling such tales. He is much too wise to marry beneath himself."

Then she stopped and drank the rest of her wine, motioning for the footman to refill her glass, although she had already consumed enough to make her tipsy.

Alicia would willingly have wrung her neck to keep this bit of nastiness from surfacing. Darcy wasn't stupid. He'd know such a rumor was being chewed over in every drawing room in Derbyshire. No man likes to be subject of gossip.

Quincy, ever deaf to nuance, not alerted by Darcy's icy mien, urged, "And what is the rest of the story, Lady Beatrice?"

She smiled smugly. "I have not yet decided, Mr. Rawson."

Ingham, remembering the lash of Darcy's anger, tried to change the subject. Finally even Quincy caught on and looked guiltily at Alicia.

Tense silence fell over the dinner table. Even Miss Austen, who was usually adept at keeping polite discourse going, was at a loss. Lady Beatrice's venom had cast a pall over the evening.

As if satisfied with the havoc she'd wreaked, her ladyship now announced that she must be off to Foxmere. "I'm hunting tomorrow. I need my rest."

Both Sir Hilary and Quincy leaped up, begging for the privilege of seeing her home. She kept them on tenterhooks while she looked first at one man, then at the other. She tapped each man playfully with her fan.

"It would seem I shall be well escorted tonight, with two gentlemen to see me home." She looked pointedly at Darcy, as if expecting him to make a third; but he refused to play her game this evening.

Alicia wasn't sure whether he was angry about the rumor or annoyed with Lady Beatrice for ruining his party by bringing it up. In either case, Alicia wasn't looking forward to being alone with him. She could see his rage building, knowing the symptoms all too well by now.

Miss Austen also murmured that she must be getting back to the Rutland Arms, as she wished to retire early. Tomorrow she must work on her novel.

Putting off the evil day as long as possible, Alicia quickly said, "I shall accompany you, Jane. It is such a pleasant evening, I'll enjoy the drive."

Darcy kept silent, only muttering a few reasonably polite words to his departing guests. The look he shot at Alicia was pure poison, though. She had a feeling he'd be waiting up when she returned, primed for a battle.

Once settled in the coach, Jane said, "Do you think he understood what she meant? I expected an explosion right there at the table."

"No," Alicia replied ruefully, "but you may hear one about an hour after I leave you at the inn. Believe me, he knew what she meant. The most provoking part of the whole thing is that his own mother started this insane rumor. Knowing Darcy, he'll blame me for it."

"Lady Beatrice may think you are the one who first circulated the story. If so, it's no wonder she's angry."

"No matter, I'll be blamed by everyone. It really was wicked of Lady Pennsfield to do it."

"She's on your side, Morgan. Her ladyship does not want Lady Beatrice to enter her family—and can you blame her for that?"

"Not for that. I do place the responsibility firmly in her lap for starting this rumor. Darcy is furious—and who can be surprised?"

"A pretty coil," Miss Austen agreed. "Would it help to tell him the truth?"

"I doubt he'd believe me. And Lady Pennsfield would be very angry if I gave her away. No, I suspect I'll be out of a job tomorrow."

"Oh, that's cruel!" Jane cried. "What will you do?"

"I'll manage."

"Perhaps things will look better tomorrow, Morgan," Jane said as she alighted from the carriage at the Rutland Arms. "Come take tea with me any day. I shall wait eagerly to learn the denouement of this story."

"I fear there'll be no happy ending, Jane."

Alicia wished she could prolong the coach ride forever so that she would not have to face Darcy; but it wouldn't be fair to the coachman to ask him to stay out late. As it was, the long summer twilight was gone, and he'd had to light the lamps on either side of the carriage. Luckily it was a moonlit night, so driving wasn't difficult.

As the coach rattled on, Alicia wondered if she would ever be able to extricate herself from the charade she had chosen to stage. She had gotten herself in too deep. How she wished she had paid attention when Hon Zella had advised against it!

Now that she could not salvage the situation with Darcy and faced a complete break with him, Alicia was forced to admit that he was her ideal man. He was prickly and bad-tempered at times—but then, any man would be bad-tempered, given a useless arm and an urgent task to complete. No wonder he turned savage when he couldn't write. Alicia smiled a little at the thought of Darcy's pacing the study and pouring out Lady D's extravagant prose. Writing such stuff was an odd occupation for a man like Darcy, but she had to allow that she shared his infectious high spirits when his ridiculous story was flowing well. Life with him would never be dull.

Alicia sighed and sank deeper into the corner of the coach as it approached the manor. She had built more hopes on Darcy than she had realized. He hadn't given her much encouragement, and none since Lady Beatrice had reappeared. Now everything was over.

She tried to slip into Pennsfield Manor and up to her bedchamber without having to confront Darcy; but he was waiting for her as she came in the side door.

"Trying to slip in, Morgan?" came his voice from the shadows.

"It's closer than the front door, Darcy."

"Indeed. Come into the study."

"Truly, I am very weary," she protested. "Can't it wait until morning?"

"No, it can't." There was something in his tone that brooked no nonsense. She followed him into the study. His back was rigid as a board. He moved behind his desk as if emphasizing their unequal relationship.

"Sit down, Morgan," he ordered, seating himself without waiting for her to obey.

She sat quietly, although her stomach churned with tension. What would he say? He let her stew for long minutes before he started, his voice cold and remote.

"That was an interesting story Lady Beatrice told, wasn't it, Morgan?"

"Perhaps Lady Beatrice should try her hand at writing fiction," Alicia replied, trying to mask her distress with a flippant manner. "Maybe the two of you could collaborate on a story."

"Ah, but Lady Beatrice isn't the storyteller, is she?"

"She seemed to be doing a creditable job tonight." Alicia subsided, too disheartened to fence with him. Let him say what he had to say and be done with it.

"I assume this charming little tale has made the rounds of every drawing room in Derbyshire."

"How should I know? I don't frequent drawing rooms. I'm a secretary."

"Yes, a secretary. With designs on her employer, it would seem."

Alicia rose swiftly to her feet, eyes flashing dangerous fire. "How dare you assume that I started this vile rumor."

"Then you have heard it? Why didn't you tell me?"

"Because I knew you would be furiously angry. Now, good night, Darcy. I'm tired and I don't care to discuss this further." She turned and walked toward the door; but he was there before her, back to the door, eyes glittering.

"As you have just reminded me, you are my secretary. I have not yet dismissed you, Morgan."

She wanted to slap his smug face.

"Very well, what else do you want?" she demanded.

"I want to know where this rumor started."

"Don't look at me. Surely you don't think I'd suggest to anyone that I was such a jobbernowl as to wish to marry you."

"And what's wrong with me?" he asked, voice dangerously low.

"Truly, Darcy, I haven't all night; and it would take that long, or longer, to catalog your bad habits."

"You, my toplofty secretary, need to learn a few hard facts about working for someone who is your better," he growled.

"You my better? Ha!" She gave him a withering look. "Now, get out of my way. I wish to retire."

"Don't you give me orders, you—" He took a step forward, picked up her sapphire pendant and looked at it closely. "I'd swear these are real sapphires."

"So?" She pushed his hand away and retreated a little, not wanting him so close to her, for he set her foolish heart to thudding.

Darcy asked slowly, "What is a secretary doing with real sapphires?"

"I fail to see that it is any of your concern."

"It might be my concern." Darcy relaxed his stance and leaned back against the door. "You are a secretary—as you keep reminding me—*my* secretary at the moment. Now—" he smiled at her tauntingly "—how would a secretary acquire a set of valuable sapphires? Might she have acquired them from a former employer?"

It was too much. Her hand swung up, and she slapped him hard. The moment she did it, she regretted her rash action; but too late to undo the damage.

"You are dismissed," Darcy said, face white with rage except for the red mark of her hand on his cheek.

"No, I quit," she lashed out at him. "I will not work for someone who suggests that I am a thief."

"A scheming, conniving, lying one at that. Odbert will drive you to Bakewell in the morning to catch the London stage."

"Morning can't come too soon. And now you may have that hussy, Lady Beatrice, to do your writing for you, as she offered earlier. She can spread the story of your double identity all over the county. Won't they buzz in all the drawing rooms in Derbyshire when they learn you are the Lady D who writes those silly romances!"

She pushed him aside, flung open the study door, flounced out and slammed it behind her. Then she fled to her room, bursting into tears before she was up the stairs.

She was crying only because she was so angry, she kept telling herself; but she knew she was practicing self-deception. No matter what horrid things he'd said, she didn't want to leave Darcy.

CHAPTER TWELVE

"OH, MISS, are you really leaving?" Fanny asked, her plump little face distressed. "We'd all thought you and his lordship . . . well, the rumor was—"

"That rumor is a lie started by a scheming old woman," Alicia snapped. "I am not going to marry Lord Pennsfield. And you can tell all the gossips in the servants' hall what I said."

Taken aback by Alicia's scathing tones, Fanny blinked, said, "Yes, miss," and busied herself with folding Alicia's gowns and putting them in the gaping trunk.

Alicia, realizing she'd vented her anger on an innocent maid, apologized. "Fanny, I'm sorry. It's just that I am so upset. I shouldn't have spoken to you the way I did."

"It's all right, miss. When your heart is broken, you often say things you don't mean."

"My heart is perfectly whole," Alicia said, exasperated. "Fanny, I never was planning to marry Lord Pennsfield. He never asked me to. I never accepted. Do you understand? I daresay he'll marry Lady Beatrice Underhill—if she doesn't walk out on him again."

Nothing she said could change Fanny's mind. Fanny was sure that Alicia and Darcy had had a lovers' quarrel.

"Oh, miss, surely not! We'd all much rather have you as mistress of the manor. No one likes her ladyship."

"Fanny, Fanny, can't I convince you that there is nothing between his lordship and me? And there never has been. We don't deal well together. We've spent more time quarreling than we have agreeing."

"I think he's a bit chary of women since he was jilted."

"Then more fool he to take up with Lady Beatrice again."

"True, miss." Fanny nodded sagely.

"So he'll get what he's asked for." Then, to change a painful subject, Alicia took a pretty little sandalwood fan and handed it to the maid. "This is for you, Fanny."

The brown eyes opened wide. "Miss! It's much too nice for me."

"Carry it when you go out with your young man," Alicia suggested. "There's nothing quite like a fan for flirting."

The little maid rushed over to the mirror, opened the fan and peered over it at her reflection. "Like this?"

"Exactly like that."

Alicia tried to keep busy. If she allowed herself to think of the journey to London, she might burst into tears. She was going to stay tonight in the Rutland Arms, dining with Jane, who had been advised early that morning by note of the disastrous events that had taken place when Alicia came back to the manor last night. By return messenger, Jane had extended the invitation. Alicia would catch the early coach to London tomorrow. She considered hiring a post chaise so she could travel more comfortably but decided she would continue her masquerade until she was well away from Bakewell. She wasn't quite sure why she was so reluctant for the truth about her to be known.

What she'd do when she got back to her home in Berkeley Square, Alicia hadn't yet decided. After this fiasco, the thought of disguising herself once more had little appeal. Perhaps she'd travel on the Continent for a time; although every man she met there would know she was rich.

To think that she'd met a man who was wealthy, handsome, eligible, interesting—and obnoxious!

Just then there was a tap at the door. When Fanny went to open it, a footman murmured a message.

"What is it, Fanny?"

"His lordship wishes to see you in his study, Miss Fitzhugh."

"Well, I am no longer in his employ. I have no intention of dancing to his tune." Alicia went on packing resolutely, although she was dying to know what Darcy wanted.

In ten minutes, there was a thunderous knock on the door, so startling that Fanny dropped the hatbox she'd gotten from the wardrobe. Scurrying across the room, she flung open the door just as the thundering started again.

"Leave us alone" came Darcy's familiar voice.

"Yes, milord," Fanny gasped and flew from the room.

Alicia turned to face Darcy, scarcely knowing how to react. He stood in the doorway for a moment, then came in and closed the door behind him.

"I sent for you some time ago, Morgan."

"I believe you did," she said, managing to keep the quaver from her voice.

"You are exasperating!" His temper was getting the better of him.

"Don't shout at me, Lord Pennsfield," Alicia cried, her own temper flaring to match his. "I am no longer in your employ. I don't have to jump when you say 'jump' and I don't intend to."

"Never have I known a woman quite so provoking!"

"I am glad I am unique," she said dryly. "Now, if you'll excuse me, I must finish my packing so that I can leave as you requested." It was then that she noticed he had a letter in his hand. "Oh, is that a letter of recommendation for me?" she asked, bright and brittle.

He stalked over to her and shook the letter in her face. "I pity the next man who hires you," he growled. Visibly taking hold of himself, he said briskly, "Something has come up."

"Indeed?"

"This letter is from my publisher."

"He no longer wants your ridiculous romances?"

"Morgan, I warn you—" He stopped, took a deep breath, then continued more calmly. "It's just that the publisher wants a few minor changes made."

She shrugged. "So make them."

He scowled one of his superbly black scowls and glared at her. Alicia looked back, all innocence.

"How can I make changes in the manuscript when I cannot write?" he asked, carefully rational.

"I really don't know." She smiled brightly. "Lady Beatrice?" she suggested sweetly.

"Don't be a nincompoop!" He lowered his voice. "You know very well why I can't have Lady Beatrice act as my secretary."

"Because she can't spell?" Alicia asked, enjoying every minute of the exchange.

"I know you don't like Lady Beatrice."

"You are improving. Now you begin to talk sense."

"I'd like to shake you," he roared.

"I wouldn't advise it, Darcy." From every word hung an icicle.

He paced the room, looking murderous. "Morgan, you can't leave this morning."

"And why not? Have all your horses come down with the colic? If so, I am quite prepared to walk to Bakewell. I should hope you would send my boxes on whenever your cattle recover—"

"Will you be quiet? You can't leave because I need you here."

"I can't be bothered with a man who says 'go' one day and 'stay' the next. Maybe Lady Beatrice puts up with—"

"Why don't you stop throwing Lady Beatrice in my face?"

"But I thought you were interested in her."

He didn't answer, but his scowl was so black that Alicia felt she needed a pail of whitewash to lighten his countenance.

She turned and put a scarf in her trunk.

"Stop that this instant!" he ordered.

"I beg your pardon. I don't like men who use that tone with me." Men had quailed when Alicia dressed them down this way.

Darcy, though, was made of sterner stuff. "Enough of this nonsense. You agreed to come here to work until my arm healed. It hasn't healed. Therefore you are in honor bound to stay."

She laughed in his face. "Indeed, sir, in honor bound? Whose honor? Certainly not yours. I distinctly remember that you dismissed me last night. Now, let me tell you a few home truths. You cannot have it both ways. If I have been discharged from your employ, I owe you no allegiance. If you expect me to drop everything and come running at your beck and call, then I am still employed by you." She gave him a very direct, challenging look. "Well, my lord, which shall it be?"

"I thought we'd agreed to be Morgan and Darcy," he said petulantly.

"Sir, you are as fickle as a weather vane in the wind."

"Oh, very well, have it your own way. You knew I hadn't really meant for you to leave."

"Did I, indeed? And why else am I packing my boxes?"

"To further irritate me, that's why!"

"Must you always raise your voice to me? I am not deaf, although I may well become so if you keep shouting."

"Well, will you stay to help with the revision?"

She gave him a calculating look. Now was the time to solidify her advantage. "I distinctly remember your implying that I was a thief," she reminded him, to his chagrin. "You seemed convinced I had stolen my sapphires—or had been given them by some man who kept me. Neither supposition is true. I require an apology if I am to stay on here."

He heaved a sigh, shook his head, muttered, but gave in. "Oh, very well. I am sorry I impugned your honesty and your virtue. There, are you satisfied?"

"I think it will do for the moment. I suppose you expect me to start work immediately." She looked pointedly at her half-packed trunk.

"Let Fanny unpack for you. We can't waste any more time. Remember, I still must complete the book by the agreed date even though the revisions will take time to do."

Alicia thought of telling him that it was silly to bother with revising such utter nonsense as he wrote, but she held her tongue. She'd won this round. Now it was wise not to rub his nose in the fact.

"I must go to Bakewell for dinner," she reminded him. "I promised Miss Austen I would join her this evening."

"Oh, very well. I shan't be here tonight, anyway. I'll probably dine at Foxmere."

So he still was chasing after that scandalous woman.

Alicia took comfort from the fact that she still was at Pennsfield Manor. And Lady Beatrice hadn't dragged Darcy back to the altar. There was still hope.

That afternoon, after she'd finished her task for Darcy, Alicia had an unexpected caller: Quincy Rawson. Strolling through the rose garden with him, she knew something was the matter.

"Are you having difficulty with your suit to Lady Beatrice?" she asked. She still thought her best chance was to remove Lady Beatrice from the running, and she hoped that Quincy and Hilary Ingham would be her means for doing this.

"It's not that, Lady Alicia." At her warning look, he shook his head sadly, earnest blue eyes mournful. "I'm afraid I've let the cat out of the bag to Ingham."

"Which cat, Quincy?" But she knew. She'd been afraid of this from the moment she saw Quincy at Chatsworth.

"He was talking about you—about how surprised he was to discover you were a mere secretary. Well, it just slipped out, Alicia."

She sighed. "You told him my name?"

"No, no, of course not, Alicia."

"You told him who I am?"

"Not exactly."

"You told him I'm an heiress."

"Afraid so. Look, how can I win Lady Beatrice if so many men are dangling after her? There's Lord Pennsfield, who must have the inside track, although for the life of me, I can't see why he'd run after someone who jilted him—unless his pride is damaged, and he wants to prove to himself and all of Derbyshire that he can win her back. Then Ingham is now after Lady B. He admitted to me that he'd not considered her, because she has quite a reputation, and he'd never be able to compete with Pennsfield. So I thought that if I eliminated Ingham by having him dangle after you, perhaps I still might have a chance with her." He gave her such an ingenuous look that she couldn't find it in her heart to hate him.

"Poor Quincy. Do you crave a fortune so much?"

"I know she's fast—but at least she's not dowdy. I've known heiresses who were so ugly they should have worn veils," Quincy said. "As to craving a fortune, yes, I do. Have you any idea what it's like to be a fourth son?"

She knew. The circumstances of younger sons were miserable unless the family fortune was huge. With estate and title entailed, everything went to the eldest son. Most estates needed large funds to keep them going.

"Quincy, I came here to escape fortune hunters."

He smiled sweetly. "You can always leave."

Wickedly she reminded him, "If I leave, Sir Hilary will still be dangling after Lady Beatrice." Then, in a last-ditch effort, she pleaded, "Don't tell anyone else. And ask Sir Hilary to keep my secret, too." Pleading wouldn't do any good, she knew, but she had to try. If this story moved as swiftly as the rumor of her betrothal, Darcy would hear it before the week was out. Then—ah, then the fat would be in the fire, the fur would fly, the cat would be among the pigeons. And she'd have to beat a hasty retreat to London.

CHAPTER THIRTEEN

DARCY WAS WAITING in the hall when Alicia came
down to go into Bakewell to dine with Jane Austen.
She wore a spencer of cerulean blue *soie de Londres*
over a cambric muslin round dress with puffs and a
flounce at the hem and a bonnet of white watered *Gros
de Naples* trimmed with blue tufted gauze.

"You look charming. It seems a pity to waste such
a pretty picture on a woman, Morgan."

Perhaps he would offer to drive her to Bakewell
himself. Just then, though, Vernon announced Sir
Hilary Ingham, who was right on the butler's heels.

His face fell when he saw that Alicia was dressed to
go out. "What appalling luck!" he exclaimed dramatically. "I had hoped to have the pleasure of your
company, Miss Fitzhugh."

"I am dining with Miss Austen at the Rutland
Arms."

"Then may I drive you there? I have my gig just
outside."

"My coach will take her," Darcy said shortly.

"Nonsense, Pennsfield, I'll be delighted to play
coachey."

Alicia smiled sweetly into his dark eyes, seeing a
heaven-sent opportunity to make Darcy jealous. "It

will be pleasant to have your company, Sir Hilary. Then, Darcy, your coachman won't have to come out."

"I'll have him bring you home. Will ten be all right?"

"Certainly. Thank you, Darcy." Sir Hilary didn't offer to bring her back, which was all to the good. She didn't want him joining her for dinner at the Rutland Arms, for she had many personal matters to discuss with Jane.

"Then I'll be off to Foxmere. No point in dining alone."

Sir Hilary quickly put paid to that idea. "Sorry, Darcy, old fellow, but Lady Beatrice is going to a rout with Miss Morgan's friend, Quincy Rawson."

When Alicia bade him a good evening, a tight-lipped Darcy scowled one of his midnight scowls.

As they rode along, Sir Hilary commented on Darcy's mood. "Jealous of your friend Rawson, I daresay. Lady Beatrice is playing the two of them like a fisherman playing a trout."

"I thought you were one of her admirers, Sir Hilary."

"She does have a sumptuous fortune, but she's not for me. A bit too fast for my taste."

"That's not very kind," Alicia chided. "I thought you were in the running for her favors."

"No, I'll leave her to Darcy or to your friend Quincy Rawson. I'm not sure I wish either of them luck. Perhaps the loser will be the lucky man in this case. No, dear Miss Morgan, I prefer quality. Do you recall the night I met you, I said you were quality? I've not changed my mind.''

Alicia was excessively bored and had no wish to carry on a flirtation with the heavy-handed fortune-hunting Sir Hilary, though if Darcy had been with them, she'd have been the complete coquette. She wondered what Darcy was doing.

At the Rutland Arms, Alicia insisted that she go in alone, although she thanked Sir Hilary prettily for the drive. Miss Austen was waiting for her, and Kilrock showed them into a small private dining room for their meal.

"How goes the tangled drama at Pennsfield Manor?" Jane asked as they ate a delightful repast and sipped a very good claret. "Is Lord Pennsfield going to offer for your hand?"

"Oh, Jane, I've made such a muddle of everything," Alicia cried, needing to confide in someone sensible. "When Darcy finds out the truth about me, he'll never speak to me again."

Her dark eyes calm and kind, Jane said, "Tell me about it, Morgan."

"I must. There's no one else I can trust. I'm living a lie, Jane, and I have defeated my purpose." Once the floodgates were opened, Alicia told Jane everything: her reason for fleeing London, why she pretended to be poor and the latest complication: Sir Hilary's knowledge that she was an heiress. "The only thing he doesn't know is my true name. At least Quincy didn't blab that. But oh, Jane, what will happen when Darcy learns that I am not poor Morgan Fitzhugh but wealthy Alicia St. John? He'll hate me forever."

"On the contrary, it may simplify things for him, Alicia. Ah, that is a much more appropriate name for you than Morgan. I don't believe Lord Pennsfield will marry below his station. As Morgan Fitzhugh, secretary, you would be unacceptable. As Lady Alicia St. John, you are suitable."

"What folderol," Alicia fumed. "That kind of fustian is old-fashioned."

"But very much in evidence." She smiled. "It is the same for Mr. Darcy in my story. He feels that Elizabeth Bennet is beneath him."

"But true love triumphs."

"After many vicissitudes."

"There's still Lady Beatrice."

"Where's your fighting spirit, Alicia? You love him, don't you?" She gave Alicia a knowing look. "It is very obvious."

"Not to him."

"Well, the man frequently is the last to know. Better that he should think he has persuaded you to love him. It will make him feel so superior. Men love that."

"I hate to be that kind of woman," Alicia grumbled. "My mind is as good as his."

"But, unfortunately, if you want to catch him, you must let him feel very, very toplofty."

"What will he say when he learns the truth about me?"

"By that time, he'll be so in love with you that it won't matter," Jane assured her. Her calm manner was reassuring.

"I hope so. If only I could get rid of Lady Beatrice."

"Your best card is Sir Hilary. Make Lord Penns-field jealous. Then he'll forget all about Lady Be-atrice. You know, I have been observing him, and I am sure that he does not love her. Indeed, it would be strange if he did, considering his treatment at her hands. She wounded his pride and made him look foolish. He is a stubborn man and not forgiving. I think you will find that he is overwhelming her with his attentions merely to bring her back to him. Then he can cancel his account with her."

Alicia, who had been listening with the deepest in-terest, revived. "You may be right, Jane. It would be just like him to carry out a scheme like that in secret and not even tell his mother what he was about."

"I'm sure I am," Jane replied firmly. "Now you must contrive to make Lord Pennsfield believe you are becoming attached to Sir Hilary."

"He was annoyed when Sir Hilary offered to drive me here tonight," Alicia offered thoughtfully.

"You see? Play the two men against each other." Jane paused while the innkeeper came in with fruit for them, then resumed. "Can't you urge your friend from London to court Lady Beatrice more assidu-ously?"

"She still is interested in Darcy. She keeps sending little notes to him."

"What do they say?"

Alicia shrugged. "He doesn't show them to me. I'm sure she realizes Quincy is a pauper."

"But, Alicia, she can afford a pauper for a hus-band. Like you, she has money of her own. You must encourage that suit."

"She's playing up to Quincy, but only to annoy Darcy. I think she intends to marry Darcy to spite me. She hates me, Jane."

"She's an odious woman, isn't she? I know you've said Lord Pennsfield is arrogant and that he can be caustic, but he deserves better than Lady Beatrice Underhill. His mother is right. You are much better for him than that creature."

"You know that, I know it, his mother knows it, but does Darcy?"

"I will venture to say that he does." Raising a hand to stem Alicia's protest, Jane went on. "Why has he kept you here in spite of all his tantrums and complaints?"

"Because of his arm," Alicia replied promptly.

"My dear, don't you think that a man with Lord Pennsfield's connections could quite easily and quickly have found some impecunious young man who would deal with his correspondence?" Jane smiled triumphantly.

Alicia choked back her reply. Not even to Jane would she betray Darcy's secret.

But Jane had given her something to think about. Was Darcy's need for secrecy the only reason for his making her stay at Pennsfield Manor even after they had had such violent quarrels? He had sworn her to secrecy and relied on her word that she would not betray him.... But if he had really wanted to be rid of her, he could have extracted the same promise from another—clergyman, perhaps.... No, no, this was just wishful thinking.

Alicia's thoughts were in a turmoil as she left the Rutland Arms to return to Pennsfield Manor. Kilrock had come in to tell her that her coach was waiting.

"Good luck, Alicia," Jane said. "Keep your courage high. You will win in the end."

"I hope so." She thanked her hostess for a delightful supper, then went out into the night. Instead of the coach she expected, she saw only a highflyer phaeton with Darcy's matched team in harness.

"Did you have a pleasant dinner?" It was Darcy himself.

Although her heart sang, Alicia schooled her voice to be only polite. "Very pleasant, thank you. I scarcely expected to find you here, Darcy."

"It's a nice night. I was restless, so I sent the coachman to bed. Come along, Morgan. It's growing late."

He handed her up into the high seat, then sat beside her. Tonight he didn't offer her the ribbons but drove one-handed; but he held the team to a reasonable speed, unusual for him.

"I am glad to see that Ingham delivered you safely" was his opening remark as they rolled along toward the manor.

"He's quite a reliable whip, Darcy," she said, teasing. "I never was in danger for a moment."

"That's not what I meant, and you know it. Truthfully, Morgan, I don't understand his interest in you."

"Darcy, you have a positive genius for saying things to deflate my pretensions. I hadn't realized I was so repulsive."

"That's not what—oh, what's the use. No matter what I say to you, you always take exception to it. Go ahead. Ruin your life. See if I care."

"Now I'm intrigued," she said, glad the dark hid her smile. "How am I ruining my life?"

"Ingham is nothing but a fortune hunter."

"Then why is he paying attention to me?" she asked, all sweet reasonableness.

"That's the question, isn't it? Now, no more of your setdowns, Morgan. I do not mean to imply that you are unattractive. You know very well that you are a very beautiful woman. Any man would be pleased to pay court to you."

"Except Sir Hilary?" she prodded.

"It is not in character for him. He's just hanging on by the skin of his teeth at Ravenswood. He must marry money."

"Love doesn't enter into it?"

"Not with Ingham. It can't. If he marries someone poor, no matter how delectable she might be, he'll lose the estate. I can understand his pursuing Lady Beatrice. I cannot understand why he dangles after you. It doesn't make sense."

It made every kind of sense, and Alicia feared that Darcy's mind would soon grasp this. Lady Pennsfield suspected who she was. One hint from mother to son, and she was lost.

"Morgan, I don't want you to see Ingham again."

"I beg your pardon!"

"He's not for you. You deserve something better than an impoverished nobleman." A sly note crept into his voice. "If you marry Ingham, you might have to sell those magnificent sapphires."

"Love is more important than jewels, Darcy," she chided.

"Love! You can't love that money-hungry—I won't have it, Morgan. I will not have it. You can't even consider marrying Sir Hilary Ingham."

"I thought you were friends."

"It's because we are that I know his character. He is not for you. For one thing, you'd crush his spirit in a week!"

Alicia laughed so loudly that she started the horses.

"It's no laughing matter," he said severely. "You need a strong-willed man, one who won't let you rule him."

"Indeed! And where am I to find this sterling character?"

"Don't be coy with me, Morgan. You know who I mean."

"Surely not Quincy. He's as poor as Ingham."

For answer Darcy pulled up the team and said, "I'm talking about myself and you know it, so stop playing games with me."

Alicia was, for once, speechless. Could she have heard correctly? Was Darcy offering for her hand?

"Well, what do you say, Morgan?"

"I—I scarcely know what to say," she murmured. She loved him and wanted to marry him. He'd made no mention of love; maybe he had in mind another kind of arrangement. "Are you asking me to be your mistress?" she asked bluntly.

"Woman, what is your trouble?" he shouted, waking a perching bird, which twittered uneasily in the hawthorn hedge. "I want you for my wife."

"Me?"

"I am not talking to the horses, Morgan. I know it isn't the most suitable marriage—"

"I resent that," she snapped. "What's wrong with me?"

"You are impossible," he retorted. "I can't even propose honorable matrimony to you without having you up in arms."

"I want to know what is unsuitable about me," she pressed.

"I had always planned to marry someone of my own station. It makes for a smoother life, no matter what fanciful stories your friend Miss Austen pens about mingling of classes."

"And I'm not good enough for you?" Her voice was dangerous.

"Morgan, let's start again," he begged, sighing. "I have fallen in love with you and I want to marry you. Isn't that enough? Must we quarrel even about this?"

"I'm sorry to be such a prickly character," Alicia said. "Darcy, I am honored that you wish me for a wife."

"But will you marry me?"

Sweet peace stole over her. At last she'd found the man she sought, one who loved her for herself, not for her fortune. "Yes, Darcy, I'll marry you gladly," she whispered.

His kiss shook her to the foundations of her being. Then he slapped the reins, and they rolled toward the manor.

"I'll tell Mama tomorrow. She'll be shocked, but I know she likes you."

Now Alicia was in a quandary. Was this the time to tell him who she really was? She shied away from the truth. Tomorrow would be soon enough. She still feared Darcy's reaction to the news that he was marrying an heiress who had tricked him for weeks. Surely, if he loved her, it wouldn't matter to him now.

Still, she worried and chose to remain silent.

CHAPTER FOURTEEN

IN A HAZE OF BLISS, Alicia dressed to go riding with Darcy. They had worked as usual that morning. Darcy thought it seemed wrong for her still to be acting as his secretary, but Alicia pointed out that no one else could substitute for her. She didn't mind helping him. She even refrained from commenting on the quality of the novel. Perhaps, after they were wed, she could exert subtle influence on his work to improve the literary aspects of his Lady D stories.

They were just riding out when they saw another horseman approaching. "Bother! It's Ingham," Darcy said. "Well, I intend to tell him you're now out of his reach, Morgan. He can go back to pursuing Beatrice."

Alicia carefully refrained from comment. She'd won Darcy away from Lady Beatrice. If she gloated, she must do it in private. The sooner that lady married, the better; for although Darcy had made it plain that he preferred Alicia, still she felt Lady Beatrice was a threat to her newfound happiness.

"I say, Pennsfield, must you always be occupying Miss Morgan's time?" Sir Hilary protested as he came up to them. "I'd hoped this lovely lady would go riding with me."

"I have sad news for you about this lovely lady, Ingham," Darcy said with relish. "This lovely lady has consented to become my wife. So she no longer is available to go riding with you."

Sir Hilary struck his forehead dramatically with the back of a gauntleted hand. Alicia hid a merry grin. Ingham could have gone on the stage with his dark, burly good looks and flamboyant manners.

"How dastardly of you, Pennsfield. Isn't one fortune enough for you?" Ingham cried, striking terror in Alicia's heart.

Darcy looked startled. "I'm not sure I follow you, Ingham. What's this about my fortune?" His face darkened with quick anger. "I hope you are not suggesting that Morgan is marrying me for my money!"

"Good God, no, Pennsfield. I'd never insult such a lovely creature as Miss Morgan."

"Then what do you mean?" There was something in Darcy's voice or the sudden tensing of his body that communicated itself to Rebel, who moved restlessly until Darcy hauled up short on the bridle with his left hand.

Knowing now what was coming, Alicia wanted only to use her crop on Flower and race away from impending disaster.

"I'm sure Sir Hilary is only quizzing you, Darcy," she said, hoping to turn aside the questions.

Darcy gave her a quick, shrewd look. He'd not be deflected by her.

"Come, come, Ingham." His voice was hard as flint. "What's this you're blathering about—one fortune?"

"I wasn't supposed to mention it," Ingham mumbled, turning his gray gelding's head and starting away.

"Not so fast, there, Ingham." Darcy's voice rang out loud and clear. Even Ingham recognized the tone of command and pulled up. "I demand an explanation. You have hinted something—either that Morgan is marrying me for money, or . . . what?"

With a despairing glance at Alicia, Sir Hilary wilted. He was no match for Darcy. "Surely you know, if you're marrying her," he whined, now refusing to look Alicia in the eye.

Darcy set his jaw. "Tell me, Ingham. If you don't—"

"Everyone knows she's an heiress!" Ingham cried hastily. Darcy's temper was well known throughout Derbyshire.

"And of course you wanted her for her money." Darcy's voice was scathing, his look withering. "I think you'd better leave now, Ingham, before I lose my temper."

"Uh, of course. Right away." He put the spurs to the gelding and galloped away.

Alicia expected Darcy's wrath to descend on her immediately. To her surprise, he shook the reins, and Rebel walked down the drive, with Flower following meekly behind. Maybe he'd already known about her. It would be like Darcy to learn her secret and not let her know he'd found it out. They cantered along, and she began to relax. He knew now, and the heavens hadn't fallen. Everything was going to be all right.

He turned off through a copse of oak and beech, not doing anything foolish, as if remembering that he still had an arm in a splint. Not for much longer, though. Thank heaven he had declared himself before she had to leave.

The day was lovely, and she forgot her fears and began truly to enjoy the ride. Summer wildflowers brightened the greens of grass and hedge, a soft breeze blew out the gauze veil of her riding hat, and all was well in the world.

They came to a grassy clearing with a brook gurgling along one side of it. Darcy reined in, turned and said, "Shall we rest for a while, Morgan?"

"It looks very peaceful here," she agreed.

They tethered the horses to low bushes and then sat on a mossy boulder beside the babbling stream.

Alicia drew off her Limerick leather gloves and dipped her fingers into the cool water. Then Darcy took her hand in his, and the warmth and strength of it gave her untold pleasure.

"I've always thought of you as a woman of mystery, Morgan," he said quietly. "That gets a man's attention. Do women deliberately make themselves mysterious to attract a husband?"

"Perhaps some do. I daresay most women do it unconsciously."

He gave her a look that was not very reassuring. Although his manner was calm, Alicia sensed turmoil just below the surface. Was he hinting that he knew her secret? Should she tell him now?

"Morgan, why have you played me false?" he asked in an almost plaintive tone.

Her throat constricted and for a moment she was unable to answer. She had waited too long. Now nothing she said would be right.

Still, she tried to brazen it out. "Played you false? How can you say such a thing to me?"

He dropped her hand as if it were a glowing coal. "So that's to be your attitude! You'll still pretend nothing is amiss? I'd hoped for better than this from you. I should have known. My eyes were blinded by foolish love. I do seem to make a fool of myself when it comes to women, don't I? First I choose Lady Beatrice—now you."

"Don't you dare compare me to that—that—"

"In a way she's less reprehensible than you, my dear Morgan. At least she is what she is—no pretense. I knew before I was left at the altar what she was, and I chose to ignore it. Very well, she jilted me. But I went into that liaison with my eyes open. With you, I let my love rule my head, and once again I'm to don fool's motley."

"Darcy," she cried, "you can't mean these terrible things you're saying to me. I thought you loved me. I love you."

"Do you? Ha! You enjoy toying with me the way a cat toys with a hapless mouse before it delivers the coup de grace." Once again he picked up her hand; he studied it as if he'd never seen a woman's hand before. Then carefully he laid it back down in her lap. "Such a pretty hand, graceful, capable. Who would suspect that it hid such sharp claws?"

"I should have told you sooner."

"Indeed you should have. I daresay you have some sly reason for not doing so."

She pleaded with him, then, throwing pride to the winds. "I was afraid you'd no longer want me if you learned I'd tricked you."

"How very astute of you, my dear. You do seem to read character exceedingly well." His voice was cold, cutting. "Perhaps the thing that galls me most is knowing that others were aware of this. I was the last to know." This was said so bitterly that tears came into Alicia's gray eyes. He noticed, and they seemed to feed his anger. "Tears now? What a consummate actress you are. You should be on the stage. That young actor—Edmund Kean?—could have you for a leading lady. His fortune would be made."

"Won't you let me explain, Darcy?" she begged.

"I don't need your explanations. Once I stopped looking at you through a rosy glow and let my mind get to work, I think I pieced the sordid story together quite cleverly. So many signs, but I ignored them. I remember that first evening when Sir Hilary came unexpectedly for dinner and was immediately attracted to you. That should have alerted me. Ingham has an uncanny nose for money, unerring ability to seek out heiresses. But I needed a secretary, and there you were, your references impeccable—and cleverly written to conceal the fact that you were a woman, not the man I expected. And there have been so many other little hints I ignored."

"Such as my sapphires," she said bitterly, knowing she had lost him.

"Yes, those sapphires. And your sumptuous wardrobe, which suddenly appeared in a trunk from London."

"You chose to think the worst of me then—you assumed I'd been some rich man's toy," she spat at him. "And you choose again to think badly of me."

"Ah, injured innocence. Spare me your histrionics, Morgan—or should I call you Alicia?"

She closed her eyes and took a deep breath. Then she opened them and looked deep into his cold, cold blue eyes. "So you know everything. I suppose you wormed the information out of that weak-kneed Quincy Rawson."

"Rawson? I've not seen him. Nor did I find out from Ingham. All I learned from him was that you have a fortune. Once I knew that, little things that had puzzled me began to make sense. Your manner. Obviously, you are a member of the ton—that was the thing that puzzled me from the very start—but I assumed that you'd fallen on hard times. Breeding shows, Lady Alicia."

"Then how is it that you know my name?"

"I have been pondering over you while we rode. There's nothing like a good ride to clear the brain, Alicia. Incidentally, that name suits you much better than Morgan. Where did you find such an uncommon name to use for your deceitful masquerade?"

"I'm surprised you've not found that out, too." Hurt and angry, she made to get up. She'd ride back to the manor, have Fanny pack, and hire a post chaise to take her to London.

Darcy was having none of it, though. He caught her wrist and kept her sitting beside him. "You'll hear me out," he snarled. "I remembered those two glowing letters you had. One from the Honorable Gisella Montague, my mother's friend from long ago. And the other from a Lady Alicia St. John. To these I added the *on-dit* my mother read to us from the London *Gazette* about the heiress who had disappeared from sight. One Alicia St. John, goddaughter of the Montague woman. It all fell into place."

"I don't deny it, Darcy. I am Lady Alicia Morgan Fitzhugh St. John. Don't you understand why I came here?"

"To torment me," he riposted, eyes flashing lightning.

"Don't be ridiculous. I didn't even know you existed when I answered that advertisement. You have the temerity to complain that I came incognito. And what of your own actions? You hid behind your valet's name. And speaking of deceit—we have Lady D, novelist. Even your own mother doesn't suspect that you lead a double life. If she knew, she'd probably suffer an apoplectic stroke. I know what she thinks of your so-called literary outpourings. Don't you talk to me of deceitful masquerades and hidden identities. You are just as bad as I. All I wanted to do was to rid myself of fortune hunters. I wanted to find a man who could love me for myself without being blinded by my money. Do you know how dreadful it is to question the motives of every man who courts you?"

"Poor little rich Lady Alicia." His tones were scathing. "You do not have my sympathy. You've played me for a fool and I am supposed to forget it? Never."

He got up, mounted his horse and prepared to leave her. Not, however, without a parting thrust. "And don't think to go running off to London with tears streaming over your pretty face. You've made a bargain with me to do my work until my arm is healed, and I shall hold you to it. The moment my book is finished—or my arm is healed—then you may go to London, to the Continent, to the devil, for all I care. I'm off to Foxmere."

He shook the reins angrily and cantered away.

Alicia wept bitterly. Her life was ruined, and it was all her own fault. Finally she wiped her eyes, bathed them with a dainty cambric-and-lace kerchief that she dipped in the cool, limpid stream, and got up to leave. She'd not go back to Pennsfield Manor immediately. She needed the good, sane advice of her friend Jane Austen.

CHAPTER FIFTEEN

ALICIA WATCHED from her window until she saw
Darcy drive off in his gig, probably bound for Foxmere. Then she hurried down to his study. If anyone
found her there, she would pretend to be copying what
he'd dictated that morning. Now she hurriedly went
through the drawers of his mahogany desk, hoping
she'd find one of Lady Beatrice's little notes. If she
couldn't find one, then somehow she must intercept
the next one that came from Foxmere.

Yesterday Jane had not offered sympathy. Instead,
she had given Alicia a plan to follow.

The plan required Quincy Rawson's cooperation.
Alicia planned to blackmail him into helping, if need
be. He'd given away her secret and caused her heart-
ache. Now he must play the gentleman and fall in with
her plan. Actually, it was to his advantage, too. Alicia
was going to urge Quincy to elope with Lady Beatrice. First, though, Darcy must catch them in a
compromising situation. Then Quincy must insist on
saving her reputation by marrying her. Alicia was very
cynical about this whole plan. Lady Beatrice had no
reputation to save. She hoped, though, that Darcy
would make a final break with her and Lady Beatrice

would settle for Quincy rather than have no husband at all.

Then, she hoped Darcy would turn back to her. If not, Jane suggested giving him a gentle nudge by playing up to Sir Hilary. He, too, had let out her secret to Darcy.

"You must be ruthless, Alicia," Jane insisted, dark eyes gleaming with fun. "Use both of these men. Tell yourself they betrayed you, that you owe them nothing, they owe you much. Remember, all's fair in love and war."

"And this is war?" Alicia asked wryly.

Now she searched frantically for a note from Lady Beatrice to Darcy, for Alicia's new role was forger. "I'm not at all sure I can imitate someone else's hand, Jane," she protested when the plan was put forward. "I've never seen her writing."

"If necessary, send her an invitation to tea. She'll have to answer you."

"Not necessarily. She does not always play the social game according to the prescribed rules of etiquette."

"Don't put so many barriers in your path, Alicia."

So now she was hastily searching the drawers of the desk. Ah, was this one? She took a small folded sheet of paper from the drawer, and a faint rose scent filled her nostrils. She opened it, glanced through it. Yes, it was from her ladyship. She wrote a breezy hand, signing herself only "B." After much practice, Alicia thought she could manage a fair forgery.

After some thought, Alicia decided to revise Jane's plan. She would not take Quincy into her confidence, as he'd proved to be a very broken reed. No, she'd send him a note suggesting that he make an assignation with Lady Beatrice at 2:00 P.M. the next day at her hunting lodge. Fanny had told her about the lodge when in one of her gossipy moods. Its location was well known, and so was Lady Beatrice's habit of entertaining her lovers there. Alicia would caution Quincy to be mysterious, so that the lady would go out of curiousity to the lodge. Then it would be up to him to be masterful, make love to her, persuade her that he was the man for her, not Darcy. She hinted that Lady Beatrice would welcome his advances, fibbing and telling Quincy that when she and her ladyship had exchanged girlish confidences, Beatrice admitted that she secretly adored Quincy and was playing up to Darcy only to make Quincy jealous.

Before she could get cold feet, Alicia penned this note and paid one of the stable lads two pence to deliver it to the house where Quincy was visiting.

Committed now to the plan, she practiced forging the letter to Darcy, hoping the wording would make it sound like one of Lady Beatrice's usual notes. She dashed it off quickly, lest she lose her nerve.

Alicia had told Quincy to beg Lady Beatrice to meet him at her hunting lodge in the beech copse next afternoon at two. Darcy's invitation, purportedly from Beatrice, was for three. By the time Darcy arrived there, Alicia hoped Quincy and Lady Beatrice would be in a compromising position.

It was a terrible gamble. Alicia knew she must be present too, well hidden, to see how the game played out. She would get Darcy's permission to go riding alone tomorrow.

Alicia put Darcy's note from Lady Beatrice on his desk, knowing he'd find it. Then she reconsidered. It mustn't be there until tomorrow. If he'd just come from seeing Lady Beatrice, he might suspect a hoax. She would slip it into the study tomorrow morning.

Later she was asked to attend on Lady Pennsfield in the morning room, where she found her taking tea.

"So, you are actually Gisella's goddaughter" was her greeting. There was a gleam in the sharp old eyes. "I knew I was correct in starting that rumor about you and that stubborn son of mine."

Alicia sighed as she accepted a cup of tea. "Ma'am, I fear your plans have gone awry. His lordship found me out before I told him the truth, and it has driven him back to Foxmere."

"Oh, fie! I won't have it. You are excellently suited to becoming Lady Pennsfield." She set down her tea-cup with a little clink, folded her hands resolutely and continued, "I shall have to speak to Darcy."

"Please, ma'am, do nothing of the kind!"

"I did so hope he'd choose you."

"He did, but unfortunately, before he knew of my masquerade. When he found out, he was quite horrid to me, I assure you."

"But you're still here," Lady Pennsfield said with pleasure. "If Darcy were truly angry with you, he'd have sent you packing."

"He still needs a secretary." It was a dreary admission.

"Stuff and nonsense, Lady Alicia. It means he wants you here. He's too proud and too stubborn to admit it, that's all. Just like his father." She gave a smug little smile. "But I always could wheedle him around to my views."

"Well, I can't wheedle Darcy. We're like flint and stone."

"It will make for an interesting marriage."

Nothing Alicia said would change her mind; but Lady Pennsfield did agree not to interfere. Now Alicia could only hope her plan would work.

Next day it seemed to be going like clockwork. She put the bogus note on Darcy's desk, slipped away until she saw him enter his study, gave him a few moments to find the letter, then went in to take dictation. He was just folding the note as she entered.

"I shan't be here this afternoon, Alicia. You can finish whatever we do this morning, then amuse yourself." He looked daggers at her. "Perhaps Sir Hilary will call."

She didn't answer that. Instead, she asked, "Do you mind if I ride out for a while on Flower?"

"As you like. If you want a groom to accompany you, speak to Odbert. He'll make the arrangements."

By a circuitous route, Alicia rode to the pretty little hunting lodge on the edge of the Foxmere estate. She dismounted some distance from it, tied Flower where she could crop grass, and stole through the copse until she had the front door of the lodge in view. Two horses were tied nearby.

She wasn't close enough to hear anything. Perhaps it was just as well, she consoled herself. She could only hope that affairs had progressed to a suitable stage of passion by the time Darcy arrived. If he found his lady love and another man chastely drinking tea, then all of Alicia's plans would be for naught.

She glanced at the little gold watch suspended from a chatelaine pinned to her riding jacket. Today she'd worn a soft brown color so as to blend with the scenery. She would hardly do her cause any good to be caught by Darcy spying on him. It was nearly time for his rendezvous—and even as she thought of it, she heard the sound of hooves approaching. Soon Rebel came in sight with Darcy riding. Alicia eased back, fearful of discovery, but she was close enough to hear Darcy's exclamation of annoyance when he saw two horses tied outside the lodge. What if he chose not to interrupt Lady Beatrice's tête-à-tête and rode away? He dismounted, tied Rebel nearby, then hammered on the door with the stock of his riding whip.

Even from where she was hiding Alicia could hear sounds of alarm from inside the lodge. Darcy pounded on the door again and shouted, "Who's in there with you, Beatrice?"

Without waiting for an answer, he turned the doorknob, and the door swung open abruptly. Alicia had chosen her site well. She could see into the lodge as if she were in a box at the theater. The scene was farce. Lady Beatrice was holding a gown in front of her, and Quincy, clad only in trousers he was clutching at the waist with one hand, was trying to leave through the window.

The dialogue was as bad as anything Darcy had written as Lady D.

"What's going on here?" he thundered, striding into the charming little salon. With one look he took in the velvet couch with articles of abandoned clothing on the floor beside it. There was no question what the two had been doing.

Alicia grinned wickedly. It was working out splendidly, just as Jane had said it would. Now for Quincy to make his big, noble gesture, offering marriage to restore Lady Beatrice's honor. That would take Lady Beatrice out of the running nobly. Alicia could concentrate all her efforts on winning back Darcy's love. Jane thought she could do it. Lady Pennsfield was on her side. With such a trio of women at work, how could Darcy resist her?

Now, though, she had to watch the finale of the drama that was taking place before her eyes.

"Darcy! I didn't expect you!" cried Lady Beatrice, sidling back toward the couch so that she could sit down and conceal her naked behind. However, she wasn't making very much of an effort to hide her ample bosom with the dress she held up negligently in front of her. Her blond hair was down in charming disarray.

In answer to her exclamation, Darcy said coldly, "It is very evident, madam, that you do not expect me yet. I had meant to arrive exactly in time for our rendezvous. Forgive me for arriving early."

"What rendezvous?" both Lady Beatrice and Quincy cried in chorus. "There's some mistake."

"Indeed there is." Darcy was furious. Alicia could tell by the set of his shoulders, by his rigid back, by his frigid tones.

Alicia looked to Quincy to speak up, but instead he stood immobile, his bare toes curling into the Turkey rug, and looked frightened.

"Well, Mr. Rawson, what have you to say for yourself?" Darcy demanded, striding over to confront him. Quincy cringed as if he expected Darcy to use his boxing prowess on him. What kind of ninny was he, anyway, to fear a man with only one usable hand?

Suddenly, he seemed to remember that he was a man. Blustering, he said, "Lady Beatrice and I had a private rendezvous. How dare you burst in on us this way? Why not leave like a good fellow?" Quincy gained confidence with each word he spoke. "Obviously the lady prefers me to you." He swaggered over to Lady Beatrice, forgetting that his trousers weren't buttoned properly. His confidence dwindled as he felt them slipping. As he made a grab at the waistband, Darcy acted.

Catching the fingers of his glove in his teeth, he tugged it off. Then, with the gauntlet held securely in his left hand, he once again confronted the farcical Quincy and struck him in the face with the glove.

"I'll have satisfaction for this insult and for your abominable behavior toward Lady Beatrice," he thundered. "Have your seconds contact me, Mr. Rawson."

Then he turned and marched out of the lodge.

Behind him, Lady Beatrice chortled, "A duel! In my honor! How exciting! But, dear Quincy, you must be very good. Darcy is a crack shot, even when he shoots left-handed."

Darcy mounted Rebel and galloped off, his face white with rage. Alicia crept back to where she'd tethered Flower, her clever plans in rubble about her feet. A duel! Good God, that was the last thing she'd wanted to precipitate. If Darcy winged Quincy or— God forbid—killed him, he'd be charged with murder. If Quincy was lucky and killed Darcy, Alicia would never forgive herself. What was she to do? A dead or imprisoned Darcy would never marry her!

CHAPTER SIXTEEN

"A DUEL? My son is going to fight a duel? Indeed, I think I shall have our physician cup him. He must be ill to think of such nonsense."

A distraught Alicia broke in, "But he has challenged Quincy. Glove in the face. Seconds. And Lady Beatrice thinks it is wildly exciting."

"Silly woman. Hasn't it occurred to her that both men may fire accurately and kill each other? Then where will she be?"

"I'm not worried about Lady Beatrice," Alicia cried, "I'm worried about Darcy. Oh, Lady Pennsfield, I've ruined everything. I should never have meddled."

"La, Alicia, if we women didn't meddle, we'd never catch husbands. Men aren't marrying creatures by nature. What they relish is the pursuit. Then the clever woman must make sure the man catches her." Her old eyes gleamed wickedly. She reminded Alicia of Hon Zella.

"How can Darcy pursue me if he's chasing Lady Beatrice?" she asked plaintively.

"Come, come. Just make him jealous. Put that excellent mind of yours to work, my dear. In the meantime, I'll also be thinking."

There was something in the way the dowager spoke that made Alicia wary. She didn't need more meddling in her affairs.

"Please, ma'am, don't say anything to Darcy," Alicia begged. "You would only anger him and make him more determined to fight."

"Don't worry about me, my dear. I've been managing Darcy since the day he was born."

Alicia took her leave, frightened that Darcy's strong-willed mother would cause further havoc if she took a hand in the game.

She walked back to Pennsfield Manor from the Dower House, pausing to sit on a sheltered bench in the rose garden. The sweet fragrance of the blossoms, the bright colors, the hum of bees and flitting butterflies should have lent a peaceful air to the day; but Alicia's mind was in a turmoil. It was up to her to salvage something from this coil. She did not blame Miss Austen. After all, she had fallen in with the plan readily.

Now she had to come up with something foolproof. Cudgel her brain as much as she was able, Alicia could think of nothing. She was going to lose Darcy, and it was through her own stupidity. Her heart was breaking, because she loved him dearly. She had thought her love was returned. Now her life was ruined.

Still, as she dressed for dinner, Alicia used every weapon at her disposal. She chose her gown with great care, donning a dress of Pomona green *Gros de Naples*, the short full sleeves covered by oversleeves of sheer white *crêpe lisse*. Her only ornament was a cameo pin fastened in the center of a *crêpe lisse* tucker. The gown was elegant but modest. Let Lady Beatrice flaunt her bosom if she wished; Alicia was still a lady.

They were not finished with the fish course, a baked turbot with shallots, when Darcy attacked.

"My mother has heard of my duel with Rawson. Do you know what she proposes to do?"

Not deceived by his mild tone, heeding only the icy blue of his eyes, Alicia murmured, "I'm sure she is distressed by the prospect of your being wounded. I have no idea what she plans to do."

He raised his voice, ire pouring forth like lava from an erupting volcano. "And just how did she learn of my duel? Answer me that?"

"Didn't you ask her?" Alicia countered. Unless Lady Pennsfield had betrayed her, Darcy could not know she had spied on him and told his mother.

"My mother was very tight-lipped about her source of knowledge. But I see your hand in this, Alicia. I keep hearing Beatrice and Rawson protesting about notes and assignations, including a note from me that I didn't pen."

She kept silent. He could prove nothing.

"So, nothing to say? Your silence condemns you, Alicia."

"I say nothing because when you are in a mood of this kind, nothing I can say pleases you."

"My fault, eh? How you love to turn my own words back at me, Alicia. I am a lucky man to have found you out before it was too late."

"And I'm a lucky woman not to be tied to someone as suspicious and hateful as you." She was determined not to let him see her cry.

"Well, my mother cannot stop the duel, because she will not know the hour or the place."

This was too much for Alicia. "She only wants what is best for you, Darcy. Why can't you forget that—that—"

"Yes?" His voice was dangerously low. "What did you want to call her? A liar, like you? A cheat, like you? A woman determined to make a fool of me, like you?"

What could Alicia say in the face of such an attack? Still, she had to do something to prevent this duel. "Very well, Lady Pennsfield cannot prevent you from destroying your life. But I warn you, Darcy, if you persist in this nonsense of fighting a duel, you will regret it. I shall see to that."

"Shall you, indeed? Now what clever scheme is bubbling about in your fertile mind, Alicia?"

She looked at him, gray eyes as cold as his blue ones, and warned, "If you persist in this duel, I promise you that everyone in Derbyshire will know that you are Lady D—beginning with your own mother, who loathes Lady D's romances."

He glared at her, jaw tightening until the muscles were knots under the skin. "You promised confidentiality, Alicia."

"You have already called me a liar. You should be glad that I live up to your estimation of my character. I shall place an advertisement in the London *Gazette*, too, divulging the secret. No doubt they will ask me to write a special article. 'I Was Secretary to the Notorious Lady D.' Or, perhaps, 'Lady D Unmasked—Writer Is Man.' That should go down nicely with the ton. It will keep them in gossip for weeks, Darcy."

A cold little smile twisted his lips, a smile with no humor in it at all. "And I shall deny it. I shall be a gentleman about it, of course. I will only hint that you pursued me to no avail, and that you made up this preposterous tale when I did not wish to marry you, having given my heart to Lady Beatrice Underhill."

"She'll make you miserable, Darcy," Alicia cried, desperate now. Oh, he could be so stubborn. She wished she could box his ears, knock some sense into that handsome head.

"And I'd be happier with you?" He sneered, wrenching Alicia's heart. "A liar? A cheat? You'd make me happy?"

She wanted to fall at his feet, beg him for love; but pride wouldn't let her do this.

"Shall I leave now?"

"And make my book late? Oh, no, you can't get away with that, Alicia."

Should she take heart? Was he saying this because he truly loved her and wanted her near him? Or was this his way of punishing her for her perfidy?

"And the duel?"

"I shall fight. Honor demands it." He gave her a barren smile. "I shall not inform you of the details. Then you cannot play me false and tell Mama. I shall fight Rawson without an audience of fond mothers and false loves."

Alicia had relied on Jane for advice. Now she must solve her own problem. She worried at ideas and finally hit on the best possible solution. She knew Quincy. He was not a strong character and would certainly not want to be killed in a duel. She must persuade him to flee, so that the meeting couldn't take place. He would require careful handling, though, for his pride might rear its ugly head at a most unpropitious moment.

If only she could persuade him to elope with Lady Beatrice.

She had thought of this earlier and discarded the idea, for Quincy was not a very good foundation on which to build her salvation. As Alicia tried the idea mentally, she was reluctant still to trust him. He really was a featherweight. That left her one possibility— Lady Beatrice. At first thought, Lady Beatrice did not appear to be a usable tool. She didn't like Alicia. She saw her as a rival for Darcy's love, and rightly so. Yet somehow Alicia must persuade her that elopement with Quincy was to her advantage.

What would persuade that trollop to give up Darcy? The answer finally came to Alicia in a moment of brilliance. If Darcy was removed from the scene and Quincy likewise, Lady Beatrice would have no man for herself. All Alicia must do was to persuade her that hers would be an intolerable position.

She rode Flower to Foxmere, following the same road that she had taken to the hunting lodge. Alicia schooled her mind to forget that disaster. Today's campaign must be a success, or she would lose Darcy forever. The thought of this was so horrifying that she was willing to do anything to keep him.

Foxmere was an old manor house built in the Tudor style with patterns of rosy brick set into the walls. The grounds were arranged in a more formal style than those of Pennsfield Manor, having been planned in an earlier age before Capability Brown worked his magic to achieve a natural appearance by artificial means. As Alicia cantered up to the heavy oak door, a groom ran out to help her dismount and lead Flower away to the stables.

She had chosen a quiet gray riding habit with a severe top hat of a darker beaver draped with a black veil. Her gloves and boots were black. Alicia wished to present an unthreatening facade. She presented a card to the liveried butler and was shown into a small reception chamber. Would Lady Beatrice be at home to her? Alicia hoped that her rival's curiosity would make her receive the hated woman who threatened to take Darcy from her.

As she hoped, the butler soon returned and said, "Her ladyship will see you in the Red Room, Lady Alicia."

The room was furnished in deep reds, which gave a gloomy cast to the entire chamber. Lady Beatrice, in a teal robe, was very much relaxed, her face smug, catlike.

"And to what do I owe the honor of this visit?" she asked. "Have you come to beg me to give up Darcy? If so, you are wasting your breath, Lady Alicia."

Although Lady Beatrice had not invited her to sit, Alicia sat down in a plain Kent chair. She would give her hostess no advantage. "I wouldn't beg you for anything," she said, voice cool and noncommittal. "I have come to suggest that you have not considered the possibilities in this situation completely. I cannot imagine that you wish to remove two suitors with one duel."

"What fustian is this? You can't gammon me, ma'am."

Alicia shrugged, the tiniest lifting of her shoulders. "I wouldn't think of quizzing you, Lady Beatrice. I only suggest that both Pennsfield and Quincy are crack shots. Hasn't it occurred to you that they may kill each other? One shot can kill a man." She paused a moment to let her words sink in, then added, "It may not be the evenest of duels. Lord Pennsfield will be shooting left-handed."

At first Lady Beatrice didn't answer. Instead, she rang for a maid and ordered wine. Finally, as she and Alicia sipped a very good Madeira, she asked, "Do you honestly think they both could die in this duel?"

"Yes."

"That certainly wouldn't suit me. I shall have to think about this. But you don't fool me for a minute, Lady Alicia. You want Darcy. I thought at first you were after his fortune. Now that I know the truth about you, I wonder you don't settle for Sir Hilary. You can afford him." She gave a sly little smile. That chilled Alicia's soul. Her plan wasn't going to work.

"And you can afford Quincy," Alicia countered.

She rose to leave, feeling she probably had not accomplished anything. Would it do any good to talk to Quincy? He was the one who stood to lose the most, for his prospective fortune flew out the window if Lady Beatrice wed another.

"Thank you for your hospitality."

"I must admit, your visit was not boring" was the rejoinder.

Still, Alicia left with a heavy heart. She felt Lady Beatrice might be willing to cut off her own nose to spite Alicia. She didn't love Darcy. She might even jilt him again if she won him.

As she rode back through the Foxmere estate, she saw another rider approaching. At first she feared it might be Darcy, who would be infuriated if he caught her meddling, but it was Quincy, who greeted her with some restraint.

"Have you heard the bad news, Lady Alicia?" he asked.

Now she could see signs of strain on his weak but good-looking face. "The duel with Lord Pennsfield?" He nodded, downcast. "I hope you are a good shot."

"I'm not so very good, you know. I shall fire into the air," he said, assuming a noble air.

"Well, don't count on Pennsfield to do the same. He's very angry. Really, Quincy, he has a formidable temper. Whatever did you do to provoke him into challenging you?"

Rawson turned brick-red and mumbled, "It involves a lady. I mustn't say more."

"Lady Beatrice, no doubt." He blushed again. "We've been friends for some time now. May I offer you some advice? Remember, I have been working for Pennsfield. I know how high-strung he is, what a vile temper he has. And he's vindictive, too, as I've learned to my sorrow. You have only one way to extricate yourself from this coil with honor—and with your life. As a marksman with the pistol, Lord Pennsfield is a nonpareil—even with his left hand.''

Quincy groaned so loudly that his mount shied. "I don't want to die so young," he said fervently. "If you have any suggestions, I'd welcome them. And it is dashed decent of you to help me, after I let out your secret to Ingham."

"All is forgiven. Lord Pennsfield was bound to find out someday. You just hastened that time a bit."

"What can I do to get out of this tangle, Lady Alicia?"

"I assume you still want to marry Lady Beatrice." If he had changed his mind, decided the game wasn't worth the candle, then all was lost.

"I love her dearly," he declared dramatically.

"Then persuade her to elope with you. Ride for the Scottish border as fast as you can, get to Gretna Green, and marry her over the anvil. I think elopement would appeal to her love of adventure."

"By Jove! Just the thing," he cried. "Why didn't I think of that?"

Then his face fell. Now what?

"It may not work," he said, hesitating. "What if she'll not have me? She may still want Pennsfield."

Alicia thought frantically. What to say? She would have to tell a huge lie, a statement that Quincy would believe she would never dare to make unless it was true. The perfect idea came to her in a blinding flash of genius.

"I—I must tell you a secret, one you may share with no one except Lady Beatrice—and only if she refuses to elope with you. This is to be your last resort."

He held up one hand as if taking an oath. "I promise to keep my lips sealed."

Alicia knew how Quincy's oaths were kept, but that didn't matter. This was one "secret" she wanted him to confide in Lady Beatrice, else it wouldn't work.

"Lady Beatrice can never marry Lord Pennsfield. He has a wife."

"He's married! The scoundrel! Who is the poor, unlucky lady he has taken to wife?"

"You are looking at her."

"You!" His mouth dropped open. "When did you marry him? Do you mean he is playing you false, dangling after my Beatrice? The blackguard!"

"No, no! We were married by special license last evening." If Darcy ever heard this tale, he'd never speak to her again. "Oh, Quincy, I don't want either of you endangered in a silly duel. But his pride—he'll fight, even though he no longer has any interest in Lady Beatrice. Truly, your only escape is to elope with her." Then she drove in the final nail. "If Lady Beatrice tells people she plans to marry Darcy, she'll be the laughingstock of Derbyshire."

"And I may tell her?"

"If you must to win her over to the idea of eloping."

As Jane Austen had said, all's fair in love and war.

"But tell no one else. Darcy is still very angry with you. If he should find out..." She left it to him to think of the dire consequences.

When she last saw him, he was galloping off to
Foxmere to beg his Beatrice to run away with him to
Gretna Green.

CHAPTER SEVENTEEN

ALL THROUGH DINNER Darcy fumed. He snapped at Alicia, he was brusque with Vernon and he almost reduced the maid to tears. Finally, as they sat sipping wine at the end of the dismal meal, Alicia bearded the lion.

"Is something wrong, Darcy?"

"That boor Rawson hasn't sent his seconds to me to make arrangements for the duel."

"Perhaps he thought you were joking. After all, dueling is frowned upon."

"What fustian! Isn't he a gentleman? He knows the code as well as I do."

"Perhaps he doesn't want to risk losing his life over Lady Beatrice," she suggested, not adding that the lady in question wasn't worth dying for.

"He might have sent me some word!"

Hoping that Quincy and Lady Beatrice were well on their way to Scotland, Alicia suggested, "He might have fallen ill. He might have taken a fall from his horse. Be charitable, Darcy. The man is not your equal in any respect."

He gave her a long look that she couldn't read, but said nothing more about the duel. Instead, he outlined the next chapter of his book, which they were to work on the next day.

"It's nearly finished, isn't it?"

"Yes. Two more chapters should do it."

"Then you'll no longer need a secretary." Alicia wished she'd not brought up this dismal thought.

At first she thought he was going to let the remark pass without comment, but he said, "My arm's still encumbered, Alicia. You agreed to stay until I could write again."

Her spirits soared. He couldn't hate her so very much; he didn't want to be rid of her as soon as possible. His pride was hurt. Some scheme must be devised to push him into declaring his love for her again. Perhaps when he heard the news of Lady Beatrice's elopement—that is, if she agreed to it. The most worrisome part of this whole scheme was the fear that Lady Beatrice would not succumb to the idea of racing off with Quincy to Gretna Green. Or even worse, that Darcy would find out about it before they were wed and would go dashing off after them to prevent the wedding.

She must keep him occupied. "Would you like to work on the new chapter this evening?" Alicia asked, trying to sound eager, although her hand was tired from the work she'd copied that morning.

Darcy gave her a suspicious look and she opened her gray eyes wide, the picture of innocence. "As a matter of fact, I had thought of working but didn't want to impose on you."

"No imposition at all. I have nothing else to do." *Only to keep you away from Foxmere until Lady Be-*

atrice is safely and irrevocably away and married to Quincy.

It was agreed that they would spend some time on the manuscript. Every time she had a chance, Lady Alicia would surreptitiously massage her right hand to ease the cramp brought on by so much writing. Finally Darcy caught her at it.

"You're tired," he announced.

"No, no, it was just a temporary little cramp," she insisted, loath to let him stop work lest he decide to go to Foxmere. "Your chapter is going so well. Don't worry about me, Darcy," she cajoled.

"I think we've done enough for now," he said. Then, out of the blue, he asked, "Do you play the pianoforte, Alicia?"

"Tolerably only."

"Would you play me a few songs, or are your hands too tired from writing?"

"No, no, it will be a pleasant break for me." In all the weeks she'd been there, he'd never once suggested music. She didn't know whether this was a good sign or not.

They went into the music room, a rather large room with many chairs, certainly ample for a recital or a musicale if Darcy chose so to entertain. The pianoforte was a lovely instrument, the entire case decorated with a floral design. Darcy produced some music, and Alicia was relieved to find that it was only simple airs intended to be sung. She struck the opening chords and was pleasantly surprised when Darcy sang the simple songs in an untrained but creditable baritone. Soon she joined in with her own rich contralto, and they spent a delightful hour singing the old ballads.

"We sing a fine duet, Alicia," Darcy told her when they had finished.

Her heart sang. He'd not mentioned the duel all evening, and they had spent all this time without any discord. She felt a surge of hope that everything would work out all right.

Next day they worked on the manuscript without a moment's disagreement. When they paused for a light luncheon, Vernon came in to announce a visitor.

"Ah, finally, the seconds," Darcy said, to Alicia's dismay. "It's about time. Show the gentlemen into the south parlor," he instructed.

"Milord, it is only Sir Hilary Ingham, asking in particular for Miss Fitzhugh."

Darcy's countenance darkened, and Alicia's heart fell. Truly Sir Hilary had a genius for appearing at the wrong moment.

"Oh, show him in. I daresay he'll have a bit of wine and cheese with us." After Vernon left, he added spitefully, "A free repast, no matter how slight, is always to Ingham's liking."

One look at Sir Hilary, though, and they knew he'd come for some reason other than a free meal.

"Have you heard the latest?" was his greeting as Darcy motioned him to a chair and Vernon served him with claret and Stilton.

Alicia knew what the latest would be. She only prayed that Quincy and Lady Beatrice had made the Scottish border and were now man and wife.

"You know I don't seek out gossip, Ingham," Darcy said curtly. From the way he scowled at Ingham and cast sidelong glances at Alicia, she thought he showed all the signs of full-blown jealousy, an emotion that delighted her. She smiled sweetly at Sir Hilary and earned an extra black glare from Darcy. *Good.*

"I'm afraid you've failed with Lady Beatrice," Ingham began, watching closely to see what effect his words had on his lordship.

In the act of lifting his wineglass to his lips, Darcy turned to marble.

"You've not heard?" Ingham cried happily, glad to be the bearer of this latest *on-dit*.

"We're quite isolated from the county happenings," Alicia said. "What's this about Lady Beatrice?" She knew Darcy was much too proud and stubborn to ask and she could no longer restrain her impatience. Had they eloped or not?

"Lady Beatrice and your friend from London, Mr. Quincy Rawson, eloped yesterday to Scotland to be married." He turned to Darcy, who was still a statue. "I'm sure you are relieved to have her off your hands. Not your sort at all, old man. You can do much better." Then, just as Darcy was about to answer, he added, "By the by, Pennsfield, what's this note all about?" He pulled a creased paper from his waistcoat pocket. "Can scarcely make it out. Why didn't you have your secretary"—he made a bow to Alicia—"pen it for you? That left-handed scrawl of yours is almost illegible. Something about my being a second? Sounds almost like a duel!"

"Never mind the note now. It's irrelevant," Darcy said, tight-lipped with some sentiment Alicia couldn't identify.

"You weren't going dueling, surely?" Ingham pressed.

"There's no need for a duel now," Alicia cut in smoothly, not wanting to have Darcy erupt with one of his tantrums. "He was just protecting a lady's honor. However, it seems her honor has been well taken care of."

Ingham shook his head. "Afraid I'm lost, Miss Alicia."

"It's of no consequence," Darcy finally said, but the look he gave Alicia was a long, calculating one.

"I say, Darcy, I'd like to borrow Lady Alicia if I may. Mustn't keep her nose to the grindstone, you know. Very pretty nose like that." He smiled fatuously at Alicia, who simpered in return. She didn't like women who languished at men, but her campaign was to make Darcy jealous, so she simpered and even batted her long black lashes at Sir Hilary. "I still insist," he went on, heavy-footed as usual, "she shouldn't be taking the work from some poor woman who needs to earn her living."

"You'll not have to worry for much longer, Ingham. My arm is nearly healed." The look Darcy gave Alicia was inscrutable. To her, his words were a death knell. Was he going to let her go so easily? She had to work fast to make him declare himself before she left for London.

"Well, I thought Alicia might like to go riding," Sir Hilary persisted.

"I wish her to ride with me," Darcy announced, as cold as a Scottish winter.

"No need to quarrel, gentlemen," she interjected. "We all three can ride. It's a lovely day."

Both men glowered, but both agreed. She smiled. It was working out quite nicely. If Darcy stayed angry with Sir Hilary, he'd not have time to brood over Lady Beatrice's elopement.

The ride was laughable, for the two men sniped at each other the entire time. When they got back to Pennsfield Manor, Darcy made it plain that Sir Hilary was not welcome to stay for the evening repast. Hilary, in retaliation, leaned close to Alicia to murmur, "I shall see you tomorrow," which earned him another black scowl.

Dinner was not an easy meal. Darcy attacked when they had scarcely sat down.

"I tell you again, Alicia, he's after your money."

She shrugged prettily, knowing it displayed her very good shoulders. For dinner, she had changed into a low-cut gown made of a lovely Scottish plaid watered silk. Alicia intended to use every weapon in her armory to win Darcy.

"I can afford Sir Hilary," she answered carelessly. From veiled eyes she watched him flush with anger. Good. Anger meant he cared. Indifference would be difficult to overcome. Jealousy was a very healthy emotion for her purposes.

"You'd buy a husband the way Lady Beatrice bought that fop from London?"

"If I wanted him," she said. "Obviously Lady Beatrice wanted Quincy, or she'd not have eloped with him."

"I don't care to discuss her," Darcy snarled, forgetting he'd been the one to introduce her name into the conversation.

"Shall we discuss the novel?"

"Oh, hang the novel. What do you see in this penniless neighbor of mine? I've known him a long time. I tell you, he's not for you."

"I must marry someone, Darcy," she said with all sweet reasonableness. "And Sir Hilary certainly is willing."

Darcy glared at her, threw down his napkin and stamped from the dining room.

Alicia remained at the table sipping her claret. A plan was forming in her mind. As stubborn as Darcy was, she was going to have to do something drastic to get him to propose to her a second time. What if he thought she was eloping with Ingham? Would he follow her and forbid the marriage?

A smile spread over her features. It was worth a try. She'd word her note very carefully. All she had to do was say she was off to Gretna Green. She didn't have to say she was going with Sir Hilary nor that she was eloping. She'd hire a post chaise secretly, leave the note for Darcy and head for the Scottish border alone. If he loved her, he'd follow. If he didn't—well, she had friends in Scotland. She could go visiting.

Alicia went over various plans in her mind, finally deciding she'd need the help of her friend Jane Austen to make this one work. She hurried to her room, and penned a letter, explaining what she wanted and why. First thing in the morning, she'd have one of the lads ride to Bakewell to deliver her missive and bring back Jane's answer. Her biggest problem was how to give herself a head start on Darcy before he learned of her defection. This was where Jane could be of greatest help. If she sent Alicia an invitation to dinner, asking her to come early to help her shop for a new bonnet, Alicia would be away several hours away from Pennsfield Manor before Darcy might expect her to return. When he finally came looking for her, Jane would deliver a letter from her into his hands. She remembered the occasion of her last dinner with Jane at the Rutland Arms—and hoped Darcy would come for her himself.

The scheme was a gamble, and one that might not work. Alicia only hoped that Darcy truly loved her. With this nudge, he must either let her go or declare his love for her. He had to choose the latter. If he let her go... but that didn't bear thinking about.

CHAPTER EIGHTEEN

AS THE HIRED POST CHAISE neared Macclesfield, Alicia congratulated herself on the brilliance of her ploy and hoped it was succeeding. Of course, if Darcy didn't pursue her, the plan would fail. She had wanted to get a good start. Now she must give him a chance to catch up if he was following her. She would stop at the Macclesfield Arms for a meal, then push on toward Preston while the long summer twilight made travel possible. The North Western Road was the main highway north to Scotland, going right across the border to Gretna Green. She only hoped Darcy would think she was eloping with Sir Hilary Ingham and determine to stop her. The only thing Alicia could think of that might ruin her plan was for Darcy to happen on Ingham by chance.

She tapped the top of the coach and told the coachman to stop at the Macclesfield Arms, where she would dine before going on. She was paying a pretty sum to make the long run to Gretna Green.

At the coaching inn, she asked for a private parlor, but the landlord said he did not have one to offer her.

"The best I can offer milady is a table in that small alcove by the window. I can set up screens for privacy."

Alicia, tired and hungry, agreed to this rather poor arrangement. The fare was nothing special, but she settled for the game pie, which smelled tasty.

She had nearly finished her simple meal when the innkeeper came to her, saying diffidently, "Milady, a gentleman is inquiring for you. He described your post chaise and you. He further tells me that you are Lady Alicia St. John." He was very deferential in manner. "I have not yet told him you have honored my humble inn with your presence. Do you wish to see him?"

Alicia was surprised. She'd not dreamed Darcy would catch up with her so quickly. He must have gone very early to the Rutland Arms for some reason, and Jane must have given him her note immediately. However, if he was in hot pursuit, then so much the better.

"Please show the gentleman in," she told the innkeeper. "He is a friend of mine."

When she heard footsteps, she put on her warmest smile to greet Darcy. To her consternation, the man who presented himself at her table was Sir Hilary Ingham.

"Sir Hilary! I was scarcely expecting you," she cried before she remembered she'd told the innkeeper—oh, bother! How was it that Ingham had appeared here?

"Lady Alicia! Well met!" he cried. "And thank you for inviting me to join you." He glanced at her partially eaten game pie and ordered the same, together with a bottle of claret.

"How in the world do you happen to be here in Macclesfield?" she asked, despair and curiosity warring in her mind.

"I followed you. Deuced hard time I've had, too. Where are you bound? When I saw you getting into a post chaise in front of the Rutland Arms, I assumed you were en route to Pennsfield Manor. By the time I'd gone to the livery stable and collected my gig, you were out of sight. I drove nearly to Darcy's place before I realized I'd missed you. Remembering that Miss Austen was your friend and that she is staying at the Rutland Arms, I went back and inquired after you there."

"And she told you—?"

"That you were going to Gretna Green." He looked about. "But you're not with anyone."

"No, I'm travelling alone."

A frown creased Ingham's forehead. "You're meeting him there?" he asked.

"I'm meeting no one anywhere, Sir Hilary," she said with considerable asperity. Had Jane done this deliberately? Remembering all the schemes Miss Austen had helped her devise, she could see her hand in this. Jane had sent Sir Hilary to complicate matters, or, as she was wont to put it, keep the pot boiling. If Darcy found her with Sir Hilary, then what? Perhaps Jane was right. It should make him resoundingly jealous, and as that was the whole purpose of this adventure, maybe she should thank Miss Austen for interfering.

"You're not eloping?" Sir Hilary inquired, puzzled.

"I'm not eloping."

"But Miss Austen said you were off to Gretna
Green."

"I am indeed." Then, feeling sorry for the fellow,
she added kindly, "Not everyone who goes to Gretna
Green goes there to be wed, Sir Hilary. I am visiting
friends in Scotland."

"Then there's still hope for me?" he cried dramatically.

She only smiled. Let him think whatever he wished.
Now it behooved her to delay the journey as much as
possible. If Sir Hilary persisted in accompanying her,
and she had to break the journey for the night, nothing she could ever tell Darcy would convince him that
the trip was innocent. He would think the worst of her
and Sir Hilary.

Fortunately, Sir Hilary was a good trencherman.
After the game pie, he decided he'd have some of the
joint of mutton turning on a spit, some new potatoes
and a large helping of fresh peas cooked with a ham
hock. Never one to overeat, Alicia sipped wine judi-
ciously and watched out of the window for any sign of
Darcy's arrival. She feared she had outwitted herself
by asking Jane to keep the note until such time as
Darcy came looking for her. At the time this had
seemed the best plan. Now, with Sir Hilary here, she
wished Darcy were following hot on her heels.

To prolong the meal, Alicia agreed to a sweet,
choosing a simple pudding. The time came, though,
when they could no longer stay at the Macclesfield
Arms.

"Have you bespoke your room here for tonight?" Sir Hilary asked. "I must see if the landlord can provide a bed for me."

"No, no, I plan to continue my journey while the light holds," Alicia intervened hastily. "There is no need for you to accompany me, Sir Hilary. My coachman is reliable, and is being well paid to drive long hours. I wish to keep my journey to the fewest days possible."

"No, no, I insist on escorting you, dear Lady Alicia. Who knows what terrors the road ahead might hold?"

Nothing she said could dissuade him. When he suggested they travel in his gig and dismiss the coach, she stood firm, telling him she had already paid the coachman and would rest better in the post chaise than in a light gig. Perhaps, she thought uncharitably, Sir Hilary would break a wheel spoke before they stopped for the night. Unfortunately, he'd expect her to take him with her in the post chaise. Bother!

The light was beginning to fade before they reached Wigan, and the coachman leaned down to ask her, "Shall you spend the night in Wigan, milady? We'll not reach Preston before full dark."

"I suppose it would be best." Where was Darcy? He might just now be worrying about why she'd not returned from Bakewell. She'd outfoxed herself this time. If only she had friends in Wigan, she could stay with them and not need to stop at an inn. Then her reputation would not suffer. She sighed. Why did everything conspire to keep her and Darcy apart?

They were going up a hill now, and she realized that the gig was drawing up beside them. Now what? In moments her coachman had pulled the post chaise over to one side of the road.

Sir Hilary got down from the gig and opened the coach door. "Someone's pursuing us on horseback, Alicia. It might be a highwayman."

"Nonsense. They've all been swept from the roads."

"Never mind, milady," the coachman called. "I've a blunderbuss with me. Never travel without it. A lone rider I can handle."

"We'll protect you, dear Alicia," Hilary declared.

Tired of the coach, she insisted on alighting, although both Sir Hilary and her coachman advised against it.

In the gathering gloom she could not make out horse or rider distinctly. She could tell, though, by the way the gallant beast labored up the hill, that it had been ridden hard.

Then, beside her, Sir Hilary exclaimed, "Good God! It's Satan."

Startled, she thought he'd lost his senses. "The devil?"

"No, no, that's Pennsfield's stallion, Satan. Big black brute. And I do believe it's Pennsfield up on him, broken wing and all."

A riot of emotions flew through Alicia's mind: joy that Darcy was pursuing her; worry that he'd injure himself on Satan, for he'd ridden only Rebel since he broke his arm; and finally, fear of what he'd say when he found her with Sir Hilary. She only hoped there'd be no more dueling nonsense.

The rider pulled up his winded horse and sat sagging in the saddle. Even in the lengthening twilight, Alicia could see his face was drawn and pale with fatigue.

Motioning to the coachman, she ordered, "Help his lordship dismount and watch that big brute he's riding."

"I think this time Satan's in no condition to give trouble," Sir Hilary muttered. He sounded put out and not a little fearful.

Alicia stood her ground, not going to meet Darcy, but not retreating, either. The next few minutes might well seal her fate. She'd meet it like a lady, head up, eyes gleaming. She'd not knuckle under to Darcy Cummings. He was proud, but so was she.

Before Darcy spoke to her, he gave the coachman orders to walk Satan until the horse had cooled down. Then he walked slowly over to confront her.

"You will not marry Ingham," he stated.

"I say, Pennsfield, what—"

"Stay out of this, Sir Hilary," Darcy snapped, all his anger, all his fatigue, apparent in those few terse words. "Is that your gig? Then I advise you to get in it, turn it back toward Bakewell and heard for Ravenswood. Now!"

"But, but—" Ingham blustered until Alicia intervened.

"Best do what he says, Sir Hilary," she cautioned.

"Will you be all right?"

She could see he was not loath to leave, fearing Darcy's well-known temper.

"Quite all right. Thank you for accompanying me this far."

"Go find yourself some other heiress," Darcy threw after the receding burly back.

"That was unkind, Darcy," Alicia chided gently.

"I won't have you marrying him. What's wrong with you? Are you a candidate for Bedlam, running off to Gretna Green with the likes of Ingham? You know very well I intend to marry you. Why do you always persist in doing things just to annoy me, Alicia? You are a most exasperating woman. I don't know why I put up with you, truly I don't."

A quick retort was on her lips, but she managed to suppress it. Darcy had just told her he intended to marry her. It certainly wasn't the most romantic proposal in the world. He stood before her, hollow-eyed with fatigue, and she knew by the way he cradled his broken arm with his good one that it was aching from the long ride on Satan.

Instead of giving him the setdown he was asking for, Alicia smiled at him. "Ah, Darcy, don't you truly know why you put up with me? It's for the same reason I ignore your vile temper, your bombast, your sarcasm."

Taken aback, he asked suspiciously, "And what might that reason be, madam?"

One unruly lock of blond hair had fallen down over his forehead when he took off his hat. She did what she'd wanted to do for so long—she reached up and smoothed the errant lock into place.

"The reason, Darcy? Because I love you, of course."

He stood still a moment, then threw back his head and roared with laughter. Alicia stiffened. After all this, was he only joking with her?

"Alicia, Alicia, you are delicious," he gasped as he controlled his mirth. "Truly, I think we'll deal well together if we don't take to throwing vases at each other when our tempers get the better of us."

"Darcy Cummings, I am the mildest of women," she protested, giving him a coquettish look.

"And my middle name is Calm," he riposted. Then he suggested, "As I've worn myself to exhaustion catching up with you, I think it would be charitable of you to invite me to finish the journey in your post chaise." He held open the coach door for her to enter first. To the coachman he called, "Tie Satan behind the coach for now."

Once they were on their way, Darcy said, "If it hadn't been for Miss Austen's frantic message to me, I mightn't have caught you in time. Would you truly have married that great lout, Ingham, over the anvil, knowing that I loved you?"

Alicia only smiled and didn't answer. There were some things Darcy didn't need to know.

"Well, madam, I will tell you something—and I warn you, it's the truth with the bark on it. Since you seem so determined to wed in Gretna Green, we shall continue to Scotland, and you'll take your vows with me."

"Yes, Darcy, my dearest one, whatever you say," Alicia said softly, stars of happiness gleaming in her eyes. "You know I never argue with you."

And Darcy laughed so loudly that Satan whinnied as he followed along after the wedding coach.

ATTRACTIVE, SPACE SAVING BOOK RACK

Display your most prized novels on this handsome and sturdy book rack. The hand-rubbed walnut finish will blend into your library decor with quiet elegance, providing a practical organizer for your favorite hard-or soft-covered books.

Only $9.95

Approximately 16" x 8" when assembled

Assembles in seconds!

- -

To order, rush your name, address and zip code, along with a check or money order for $10.70 ($9.95 plus 75¢ postage and handling) (New York residents add appropriate sales tax), payable to *Harlequin Reader Service* to:

In the U.S.

Harlequin Reader Service
Book Rack Offer
901 Fuhrmann Blvd.
P.O. Box 1325
Buffalo, NY 14269-1325

Offer not available in Canada.

BKR-1

WORLDWIDE LIBRARY IS YOUR TICKET TO ROMANCE, ADVENTURE AND EXCITEMENT

Experience it all in these big, bold Bestsellers— Yours exclusively from WORLDWIDE LIBRARY WHILE QUANTITIES LAST

To receive these Bestsellers, complete the order form, detach and send together with your check or money order (include 75¢ postage and handling), payable to WORLDWIDE LIBRARY, to:

In the U.S.
WORLDWIDE LIBRARY
901 Fuhrman Blvd.
Buffalo, N.Y.
14269

In Canada
WORLDWIDE LIBRARY
P.O. Box 2800, 5170 Yonge Street
Postal Station A, Willowdale, Ontario
M2N 6J3

- -

Quant.	Title	Price
_____	**WILD CONCERTO**, Anne Mather	$2.95
_____	**A VIOLATION**, Charlotte Lamb	$3.50
_____	**SECRETS**, Sheila Holland	$3.50
_____	**SWEET MEMORIES**, LaVyrle Spencer	$3.50
_____	**FLORA**, Anne Weale	$3.50
_____	**SUMMER'S AWAKENING**, Anne Weale	$3.50
_____	**FINGER PRINTS**, Barbara Delinsky	$3.50
_____	**DREAMWEAVER,** Felicia Gallant/Rebecca Flanders	$3.50
_____	**EYE OF THE STORM**, Maura Seger	$3.50
_____	**HIDDEN IN THE FLAME**, Anne Mather	$3.50
_____	**ECHO OF THUNDER**, Maura Seger	$3.95
_____	**DREAM OF DARKNESS**, Jocelyn Haley	$3.95

YOUR ORDER TOTAL		$_____
New York residents add appropriate sales tax		$_____
Postage and Handling		$___.75
I enclose		$_____

NAME _____

ADDRESS _____ APT.# _____

CITY _____

STATE/PROV. _____ ZIP/POSTAL CODE _____

WW-1-3

Now Available!
Buy all three books in MAURA SEGER'S fabulous trilogy!

EYE OF THE STORM ECHO OF THUNDER

EDGE OF DAWN

Be a part of the Callahan and Gargano families as they live and love through the most turbulent decades in history!

"...should be required reading for every American."

Romantic Times

To order all three books please send your name, address and zip or postal code along with a check or money order for $12.15 (includes 75¢ for postage and handling) made payable to Worldwide Library Reader Service to:

WORLDWIDE LIBRARY READER SERVICE

In the U.S.:
P.O. Box 1397
Buffalo, N.Y.
14240-1397

In Canada:
5770 Yonge St., P.O. Box 2800
Postal Station A
Willowdale, Ontario M2N 6J3

PLEASE SPECIFY BOOK TITLES WITH YOUR ORDER.

TRL-H-1

Six exciting series for you every month... from Harlequin

Harlequin Romance®
The series that started it all

Tender, captivating and heartwarming...
love stories that sweep you off to faraway places
and delight you with the magic of love.

◆

Harlequin Presents®

Powerful contemporary love
stories...as individual as the
women who read them

The No. 1 romance series...
exciting love stories for you, the woman of today...
a rare blend of passion and dramatic realism.

◆

Harlequin Superromance®
It's more than romance...
it's Harlequin Superromance

A sophisticated, contemporary romance-fiction
series, providing you with a longer,
more involving read...a richer mix of complex plots,
realism and adventure.

Harlequin
American Romance™
Harlequin celebrates the American woman...

...by offering you romance stories written about American women, by American women for American women. This series offers you contemporary romances uniquely North American in flavor and appeal.

◆

Harlequin Temptation ™
Passionate stories for today's woman

An exciting series of sensual, mature stories of love...dilemmas, choices, resolutions... all contemporary issues dealt with in a true-to-life fashion by some of your favorite authors.

◆

Harlequin Intrigue™
Because romance can be quite an adventure

Harlequin Intrigue, an innovative series that blends the romance you expect... with the unexpected. Each story has an added element of intrigue that provides a new twist to the Harlequin tradition of romance excellence.

Harlequin Books®

PROD-A-2

What the press says about Harlequin romance fiction...

"When it comes to romantic novels...
Harlequin is the indisputable king."
— *New York Times*

"...always with an upbeat, happy ending."
— *San Francisco Chronicle*

"Women have come to trust these
stories about contemporary people,
set in exciting foreign places."
— *Best Sellers*, New York

"The most popular reading matter of
American women today."
— *Detroit News*

"...a work of art."
— *Globe & Mail*, Toronto